HUNGRY HILL

———⋯⋯⋯⋯•❈•⋯⋯⋯⋯———

By

K. J. SARGEANT

Copyright © K. J. Sargeant 2019
This book is sold subject to the condition that it shall not, by way of trade or otherwise, be lent, resold, hired out, or otherwise circulated without the publisher's prior consent in any form of binding or cover other than that in which it is published and without a similar condition including this condition being imposed on the subsequent publisher.
The moral right of K.J. Sargeant has been asserted.
ISBN-13: 9781090308610

This is a work of fiction. Names, characters, businesses, organizations, places, events and incidents either are the product of the author's imagination or are used fictitiously. Any resemblance to actual persons, living or dead, events, or locales is entirely coincidental.

Janet. The patience of a Saint.

Karen. Your encouraging words.

Rebecca. The drama in my life.

Graeme. For your care.

CONTENTS

Chapter 1 1
Chapter 2 13
Chapter 3 16
Chapter 4 22
Chapter 5 26
Chapter 6 29
Chapter 7 31
Chapter 8 35
Chapter 9 38
Chapter 10 40
Chapter 11 42
Chapter 12 44
Chapter 13 53
Chapter 14 56
Chapter 15 58
Chapter 16 60
Chapter 17 62
Chapter 18 67
Chapter 19 72
Chapter 20 77
Chapter 21 80
Chapter 22 82
Chapter 23 84
Chapter 24 88
Chapter 25 91
Chapter 26 94
Chapter 27 97
Chapter 28 100

Chapter 29..101
Chapter 30..104
Chapter 31..107
Chapter 32..109
Chapter 33..113
Chapter 34..115
Chapter 35..118
Chapter 36..121
Chapter 37..123
Chapter 38..125
Chapter 39..127
Chapter 40..129
Chapter 41..131
Chapter 42..133
Chapter 43..135
Chapter 44..139
Chapter 45..142
Chapter 46..144
Chapter 47..146
Chapter 48..148
Chapter 49..150
Chapter 50..154
Chapter 51..158
Chapter 52..160
Chapter 53..164
Chapter 54..166
Chapter 55..168
Chapter 56..170
Chapter 57..172
Chapter 58..173
Chapter 59..176
Chapter 60..178

Chapter 61	184
Chapter 62	186
Chapter 63	192
Chapter 64	193
Chapter 65	195
Chapter 66	197
Chapter 67	201
Chapter 68	206
Chapter 69	208
Chapter 70	211
ABOUT THE AUTHOR	216

Chapter 1

The first boyfriend that Grace Buchanan ever had, proved to be a generous lover and adored the teardrop-shaped hollow at the top of her fleshy thigh. Now, many partners later, crudely forged steel jabbed at that dimple and she yearned for the lad again. The agony of it came in waves, every time she regained consciousness, then faded as the woman drifted back into a sleepy fog. In her dream, she saw wet cobbles on a street of townhouses not known to her and searching for something familiar, her eyes found a street sign attached to brickwork. The black embossed letters of STONEWOOD PARK were thick and she heard herself read them aloud. Someone else heard those words but they were too busy tightening Grace's shackles to notice.

It wasn't actually a dream; more a memory, but as real as the rain that dripped into her eyes. Some stone steps to her right were solid as well and she didn't fight an urge to climb them. At the top, a uniformed PC lifted some crime-scene tape as she reached a porchway, then ducking under it to push through a door, Grace found somewhere to lose her Starbucks. She held on to an unopened pastie, but would later offer it to the PC after suddenly losing her appetite.

Out of the rain, darkness prevailed and some potpourri next to Grace's coffee couldn't disguise the depressing stench of mildew. Reaching for the paper cup again, she heard noises floating down from one of the rooms, noises that she always thought of as a soundtrack to her young life. In the air above her, hung a forensic silence, interrupted only by the click of Pentax or the mutterings from some expert technician. Then, mindful of someone taking prints, Grace forgot about her latte and trod the stair carpet. On the landing, stark lighting greeted her and she heard her name called from behind its glare. "Buchanan... over here, will you?" Recognising the male voice, she navigated a path though some cables and found the hunched figure of Samuel Gregson.

Grace spoke while the man got to his feet.

"Is it bad?" she asked.

"Depends who you are, really," he replied. Grace looked puzzled as he continued. "If you're the person in the bedroom it's bad enough; on the other hand, if you're in the bathroom, then it is unbelievably bad." The look in Gregson's eyes chilled Grace and gave her a feeling of dropping too quickly in an elevator. She disguised it well, then stepped towards a half-open door, after glimpsing a sink, littered with toiletries, over his shoulder.

Sam Gregson's eyebrows were blond with a few greys, like his untidy fringe, and he raised one.

"Here, you might want this," he suggested, holding out a surgical mask.

In Grace's memory dream, she took the mask and stepped sideways through the door of a grimy

Hollywood bathroom belonging to a very recently dead rock star. In reality, apart from the heroin kit and white powder everywhere, it happened to be an averagely clean bathroom, in an averagely good tenement block on the east side of Edinburgh, and the averagely overweight naked body of a deceased male, slumped precariously on the toilet, had never known celebrity of any kind. Sadly, he would certainly make it onto all of the front pages by the next day.

Detective Buchanan's career in Edinburgh's metropolitan had barely started when she saw her first homicide victim, one who was unfortunate enough to have had the sharp end of some surgical scissors stabbed into their thigh, just in front of the kneecap. They were rammed so hard that only two oval handles were still visible, and Grace was looking at them now. Apparently, the steel blades had punctured a hole at the end of the femur, then self-sealed, allowing just a trickle of blood to escape down a pasty-looking shin. In the grand scheme of things, it was just a pin prick but Grace was in no doubt as to the cause of death, and it was a "Grizzly one, make no mistake." She said that to herself, in an attempt at injecting some humour into the situation. Damning evidence of it surrounded the young policewoman on every surface, then a small part of it dripped onto her index finger.

Fresh blood has a scent all of its own but not an offensive one. Often regarded as metallic in odour, a large amount of it can be quite strong. This stuff had a nauseating smell, so repellent that Grace had to pinch the mask hard, to get it even tighter over her nose. The reason for it, hung right above her head and explained the sweltering temperature. Obviously a relic from the 1970s, an electric ceiling heater, with both elements switched on, appeared to be frying the victim's ejected blood and sizzling like a kebab shop spit. The interesting part of this case, would be how the room got to be decorated in eighty percent of the man's AB negative.

The flooring was almost certainly painted boards from what Grace could make out, after crouching before John Doe to get a better handle on everything. Taking advantage of the only clean area, immediately in front of the body, Grace balanced there, focusing on the carnage that was once the man's penis. Apparently, he'd used most of his share of life's good fortune in the trouser department, though it had run out in the last twenty-four hours and a very large helmet with foreskin, suspended by a thin sinew of pink flesh, hung over the toilet's rim. Evidently, the rest of his member had taken the full impact and lay shredded against hair-covered legs. Studying the gaping hole, Grace half expected a head full of teeth and whiskers to jump out and attack her. That imaginative thought became lost, when she noticed a blotchy redness under the man's chest hair, and strangely, matted in amongst the curls, a hypodermic syringe was caught there with its needle still pricking the skin.

Turning on a boot heel, forensic protocol stopped Grace in her tracks. She'd remembered two ampules amongst all the crap cluttering the sink, and needed to see those labels. Retracing her steps too many times was asking for trouble, so using a biro, she leant over and retrieved one of the containers. By the time Grace had replaced it, she'd worked out what had led to the profusion of blood, some of which was now snaking its way down her neck. Liquid Viagra pumped directly into the heart, is not a good way to start the day, especially with a cable tie fastened tightly around your dick. Grace had found the white tie wrap accidentally, while checking out the body's bloated ankles. Then realised someone had used more of the plastic ties to link them to the man's wrists under the toilet, trapping him there. She located another one smeared with fatty tissue in his lap. At that point, Gregson stuck his head through the door.

"Pressure had obviously built up down there, big time," he offered and Grace finished his sentence.

"But with nowhere to go, a rupture occurred at the weakest point."

Gregson clicked his fingers. "And BOOM, you've got new wallpaper."

Grace hid her disgust and asked him about the chest marks. He said he wouldn't know for sure until the cavity was opened but then, lowering his voice, "I'll say this though Grace, I'm expecting to find a bit of a mess in there."

She probed some more. "His heart?"

Gregson nodded. "Yes... Exploded, I'd say."

Before Grace left the apartment, she'd learnt that the victim's name was Thomas Collins and the general consensus was that he hadn't topped himself, but that a particularly ruthless psychopath had injected the sex drug 'sildenafil nitrate' straight into the heart muscle, then placed a pair of scissors teasingly within reach, albeit buried deep inside the bloke's leg and for all the good they did him, they might as well have been flushed down the toilet. With those scissors, he might have cut the constricting plastic tie and halted a build-up of blood pressure that Gregson compared to a lorry tyre's blowout.

Behind the wheel of her little Fiesta, Grace thought about Mrs Alice Collins for a moment. Her last minutes were not quite so dramatic as Tom's, but equally harrowing and bore a second similarity. Cable ties were involved quite extensively in her suffocation but not before the perp had paid a visit to wonderland with our lovely Alice.

After reading some notes by the light of the car's interior, Grace closed her eyes for a second and was instantly transported back to those shackles again. With that reality, a searing pain came crashing in and she grasped at her own crotch. Tethered to the real world, the young woman made no such move against her restraints, but in her memory dream Grace experienced cold leather and steel, then her mobile went off. She hit the screen once, then again for speaker. From outside the car, her auburn bob took on the iPhone's red glow, giving it the eerie appearance of a futuristic crash helmet. Back inside the cabin, the glass echoed to the sounds of Glasgow.

"Buchanan, are you there, girl?"

Grace answered. "Yes Sarge, Buchanan here."

The voice, urgent but familiar to Grace, carried a warning in its tone. "You're wanted back here, bonny lass, don't dally now." Sergeant Ashton always looked out for Grace so she heeded his words and turned the ignition.

Burton Hill, built way back in 1810 and one of three police stations in Edinburgh, is part of the 'new town'. A term that always baffled Grace, when approaching its Georgian, smoke-blackened facade. Light mist had replaced any drizzle from earlier and she felt its coolness on a brass handrail while climbing the building's greasy steps. Inside, everything had been radically updated and Grace used her ID to pass through reception. Behind the help desk, Sergeant Ashton threw a look over his shoulder and told her that the chief super was waiting. Grace couldn't imagine why, so walked through her mind, searching for a reason, something… anything that she might have done in her time at Burton Hill. While torturing herself, she hung a leather jacket in her locker, checked her hair and buttoned up the top of a navy shirt.

The young constable was breaking all records today, what with her first slaying, and now she was drinking coffee while sat in the chief superintendent's inner sanctum. Conversation between the two was all very civilised but much too long in Grace's opinion, so she was on guard for any change in tack from Chief Ronson. It happened soon enough, when he mentioned her sister.

"You've got family down south, haven't you Grace?"

Using her Christian name, was an attempt at softening her up, which Grace took as a gentle dig to the ribs. Now, if she dropped her hands she'd be open to the upper cut.

"Yes sir, my older sister lives near Newmarket."

When he threw the punch, Grace was ready but it still winded her.

"You look tired, Constable. Go home and put your feet up, oh, and maybe use the time to pack a bag, you've been handed a chance to visit her."

For the first time, Grace cracked a smile but gritted teeth were behind it.

"I'm not sure I follow you, sir?"

Now it was Ronson's turn for the fake grin.

"Constable, you're being transferred to sleepy Suffolk."

Still reeling from the low blow, the only thing she could think about at that moment was the dead man on his toilet, and her face said it all.

Ronson gauged it well, suggesting that, "This might be good for you, Grace."

She could see his point, but a wee lass from the Scottish Borders... working with a bunch of carrot crunchers? Grace loved life in Edinburgh and started to think about her dear old dad. Then the chief mentioned a cold case that she'd be involved in.

Chapter 2

Some years ago

No one polished the bannister anymore but it was still OK for the boy to slide down; not today though. When the handrail reached the top, it turned right and ran past three panelled doors. Opposite the second one, large gnarled fingers gripped the balustrade and behind that door, crouching on grazed knees, the boy held his breath. Then, feeling the floorboards vibrate in rhythm with his own heart, he wet himself. Under the door, ribbons of light punctuated the shadows and appeared to move in time with the creaking. Forcing his eyes open, he saw that his little friend was there again, whiskers twitching. The brown mouse, but this time the boy had brought something. Very carefully, he placed a few crumbs on the floor inside a dim triangular slit and watched. With its body mostly in shadow, the tiny creature's front paws scratched away, constantly grooming, and its oversized ears were picked out by the orange glow.

On the other side of the door, someone else struggled to calm their breathing. Reminiscent of a handsaw on wood, the rasping sound was accompanied by something more akin to chalk on a blackboard. It came from nails as tough as antlers and on a big toe the size of a cigarette packet. Scraping a kick plate, the deeply veined foot twitched from a supply of blood pumped seven feet above, sending tremors to the frail lad cowering inside. Dampness spread under him and he studied the curious rodent as it investigated a clothes peg jammed into the gap. Then, tail dragging, our brave little fellow squeezed its shoulders under the iron block. Envious of the mouse's quiet life, the little boy almost forgot why he was in the cupboard at all, until a hole was punched through the silence, shaking the hell out of his claustrophobic world. Fashioned from thick timber, the door held fast but its jamb's loud crack resonated like the felling of a huge oak and as dust rained down, mouse and boy trembled.

After a moment, the creaking returned and the youngster put an eye to the keyhole. His view of a tobacco-stained chandelier was partly blocked by spindles but nothing else. Then came a more comforting echo. Recognising it, he counted every foot on the bare risers as each one faded more than the last. At the eleventh he knew it had passed, until tomorrow, and wiped his face with a skinny arm.

Looking down, he was amused to see a furry bottom wriggling and switched his gaze to the rusty block. Having been home schooled, he'd always enjoyed mathematics, so after glimpsing a 20lb symbol embossed onto the metal weight, he knew what it meant and casually pulled out the peg. There came a muffled squeal and the boy grinned at Mousey's busy little legs, fascinated by a bulge forming in its hind quarters.

Chapter 3

Today, nineteen years later

Erin slipped away from her boyfriend as they squeezed through a gap in the hedgerow and smiled when he offered a hand through the prickly hole. The hill's steepness surprised the couple enough for them to break into a jog on the other side so they linked hands across tufts of dry grass and ran down the slope, stopping near the bottom. Everything was in place for lovers to go strolling this afternoon. So cue pastoral countryside, cue birds singing and glorious blue sky. It really was an idyllic scene but as they rounded a bend in the deserted lane, the overhanging bow of an ancient yew tree couldn't mask the ugliness of a rotting pile of hay near some equally rotten gates.

For Erin, the appearance of a derelict farm took the shine off her mood, but Flynn Bailey thought it was 'bangin''. He liked Erin a lot but his bro Travis had a rave scheduled and was counting on him to set it up as usual. He put a tattooed arm on her shoulder and took the cigarette she'd rolled him before kissing her fingers. Pulling him closer, she helped light the tobacco using her own cigarette and Flynn mused to himself that this scouting mission wasn't too bad, from where he was standing.

He knew that Cherry Tree Farm had been empty for years and when he'd driven past a few nights ago, he'd noticed some security lights were still working. Disused buildings without neighbours were hard to come by and if they were still hooked up to the national grid, then it was game on in Flynn's world. The dodgy entrepreneur planned on waiting it out and getting a better look tonight when it was darker, he just had to break the news to his girl first.

After crushing her ciggie under a sandal, Erin let her eyes move up from Flynn's scuffed boots, past the hole in his Levi's, to his smug little face.

"Hungry Hill?" she demanded.

Flynn pushed himself forward, pivoting on a heel in the dirt, and realised that he'd been leaning against the sign.

"Oh yeah, babe, Hungry Hill!" He grinned, while gazing back up the track. "They say the hill's got an appetite, with cars in ditches and stuff, but back in the day, it was highway robbery, you know, Dick Turpin style!" Flynn tugged a vest over his mouth and mimicked a flintlock pistol with two fingers.

"Two summers ago, a couple of girl hikers went missing as well." He paused. "Never did find 'em."

Erin stood closer to him.

"Shut up." And when she said it, her nose scrunched up, making some freckles more obvious. Flynn didn't mind that at all.

He led the way again and after walking about a mile in the heat, they stopped so that Erin could remove her denim jacket and take in the view.

"We don't do this sort of thing enough, babe," she remarked, giving her sneaky boyfriend a chance to come clean, since there was no pool table in sight or cold beer on tap. These two had been together a few years now and she'd learnt to let Flynn think he was the boss of their little outfit, just now and again.

"Why not sleep under the stars, babe, like the old days!" he enthused. Erin had to laugh.

"You cheeky fucker!" she mocked. Flynn tried to feign innocence.

"What, babe?" he pleaded, stretching those tattooed guns towards her. She nestled into them, as always, and stood on his boot.

They stayed that way for a while, before setting off once more, giggling and happy in love.

"Sweet as you like," Flynn whispered, proud of his subterfuge. When they got to a fork in the road, the stunning landscape was right out of a Gainsborough painting, or even a John Constable. After all, Flatford Mill lay not seven miles north of here. Flynn climbed a shallow bank of hardened clay at the junction of the two roads and pushed a rickety gate open with his boot. It led past some thick brambles, taking him to a waist-high field of corn that shone bright in the sunlight.

Beckoning Erin to join him at the top, he noticed that kids had built a camp from hay bales, using the string-tied bundles like house bricks. The would-be architects had gone for the bijoux cube look but only managed to create an igloo of straw with their efforts. Tall and wide, the structure shimmered in the haze and as Flynn stepped closer, the dome-shaped shelter appeared to rise upwards, blocking out the sun's glare and bringing him relief from its blinding rays. A darkened entrance loomed into focus as his eyes adjusted to shadows and Flynn realised that the den had seen better days. Testing a bale with the palm of his hand, it felt dry, so crouching forward, he entered the tunnel-like aperture.

When Erin reached the gate as well, she bent over to look in as Flynn disappeared through the opening. Kneeling on the ground, she raised a hand towards the darkness. It had gone very quiet so the lass tried calling but got the shock of her life, when from back in the gloom a claw-like appendage struck out at her, ravaging at the girl's scalp and scratching at her strawberry hair. Rocking back onto her heels as a rush of hot air unbalanced her, Erin felt something race up her bare midriff. Now, whatever it was, had hooked her blouse and she heard it rip as the thing used the girl's breast to launch itself skywards.

The unearthly shriek that filled the young woman's ears sounded more like desperation than predatory hunger and as the attacker's warm body pressed hard against Erin's face, its breath blew hot on her neck. Then, with her eyes still shut, something grabbed firmly at her flailing biceps. She dared herself to look, slowly at first, and then squinted into the desert-like sun. Flynn was on her, shouting wildly. Erin thought she heard the word 'PHEASANT'.

He spat the words out again. "IT'S JUST A PHEASANT, BABE."

Chapter 4

Five miles away, in Bury St. Edmunds, Dominic Thorndyke had just left his final call of the week. Mrs Jackson was comfortably sat in front of her television for the rest of the afternoon and Dominic could enjoy some days off. She was probably the easiest client that the young man cared for but, "God, did she stink!" He said that out loud, to amuse himself. Swaggering up St. John's Street, glancing through windows with not a worry in the world, it occurred to him that the people going about their business, were like bees in a hive. He sneered at them all as they dodged in and out of doorways that rang bells, zig-zagging across the pedestrianised street like demonic insects.

He preferred this route to the bus station because of its numerous charity shops and here was one now. The bell rang as he stepped over the threshold and there was a cheery smile from the old dear behind the counter. Dominic managed half a grin and hurried to the quiet end of the store, where novels and hardbacks were kept.

Although he was fond of reading, this corner was also reserved for second-hand clothes and that really floated his boat. Sifting through someone's personal items excited Dominic in a strange way so he used the pastime to keep his other disturbing urges at bay. One time, he slipped a grey overcoat on and casually sauntered out of the shop, with a friendly wave to the old boy at the till. Then stooping forward with hands in pockets, the loner shuffled all the way to the bus stop. Hunched over like a cripple, he observed the crowd through half-closed lids while whispering inane insults.

Silk was also a favourite of Dominic's and he came across a pale yellow scarf in that material, with a red paisley design and tassels in the same colour. Tying it around his throat, the oddball checked himself in a full-length mirror. It would clash with the dark blazer but he fastened it around his scrawny neck anyway, taking the opportunity to admire himself and buff the winkle pickers that his aunt had given him, on the back of turned-up skinny jeans.

He still had hold of both ends when the bell above the door sounded and that jolted him back to reality. In no time at all, he'd stepped behind a book cabinet and was peering over at the exit. A young woman had her back to him and was closing the glass door. Dominic rapidly digested as much information about her as he could, before she turned around. In his warped mind, the ingrate listed what was observed.

Punk type.

Long neck.

High nape where it meets short red hair. * Needs wash.

Top of arms thin but kissable.

Big gap between top of thighs. ** Two stars for that one.

Dominic always did that and when he had completed the mental notes, he clocked the old lady.

The pensioner was watching him and her eyes were on stalks. In his trance-like stupor he'd forgotten all about the scarf and had been tightening the cloth over his Adam's apple, in the fashion of a ligature rather than a cravat. Agnes had become alarmed at the sight of purple veins protruding from the young gentleman's sweaty forehead and felt quite faint.

Chapter 5

It was a good hour since the wildfowl episode and the lovers were sitting cross-legged on straw inside the camp. Erin couldn't believe that her boyfriend would possibly see the funny side of any of this, so Flynn gave her the eyes.

"Come on, doll, it was probably more scared than you were!"

"I doubt that very much." She sniffed. "Anyway, you didn't see it," she snapped back again, then laying back in his arms, she closed her eyes.

Flynn held her softly while confessing everything about the rave-farm project, tenderly stroking her hair, and she felt safe again. After some time, she tilted her head to look at him. They kissed beneath a gaping hole in the shelter's roof as sunshine streamed through above them. The shaft of orange glowed like a laser beam in a sci-fi movie and it made dust particles glisten in the air, as tiny flakes of straw sparkled all around the young couple.

It was true, that to Erin, her man was a well-read book. Mainly a tale of deception and betrayal but on the flip side of that, he himself was quite an expert on the girl lying beside him and if a coastal cliff named 'Desire' existed somewhere, then his woman stood right near the brink at this very moment. So, with controlled dexterity, Flynn let the back of his hand trace that smooth channel below her spine until it reached the crease between her muscular thighs. They pressed together in brave defiance but parted soon enough, and the eager boy found the wetness he so craved. Now, he could guide Erin to the precipice, which he did by locating her Venus piercing and then, with delicate precision, he pushed her over the edge. She tensed a little but did not crash onto rocks below, because she was soaring on thermals and her man was flying as well. So high, that he impatiently withdrew his hand and reached around, grabbing roughly at her hip. Erin knew what to do as he spun her onto those sunburnt knees of hers. While Flynn loosened his belt, she arched her back and smacked her own white arse, real hard. Then he was inside her and they were both racing towards the heavens.

Chapter 6

Back in town, storm clouds hung over St. John's Street and as Dominic stepped onto the pavement, they yielded their contents. The black umbrella from the shop would come in very handy with its usual benefits, of course, but also, like a teenager cloaked in their hoodie, the deviant was able to hide from the world and survey his turf. The little shit resented paying the four pounds but consoled himself by tightening his new scarf, which he had decided was a free gift, courtesy of Cancer Research.

When the girl had left the charity shop Dominic was after her like a lovesick kid, but without the love bit, and he wasn't going to let a little rain spoil his fun.

She'd gone into a tobacconists, as his aunt might say, so he waited under a red and white striped awning in front of the butchers. Listening for the giveaway signal from a door chime, he watched every boot, shoe and sandal that passed under his brolly with increasing fascination.

Chapter 7

In another area of town, at the end of a quiet cul-de-sac and high up in the canopy of a mature horse chestnut, a trickle of rain had found its way through some damaged tiles on the roof of number 25 Battersea Gardens. Snaking its way inside and down the crumbling lathe and plaster, it entered the attic and settled on floorboards in an ever-expanding puddle surrounding a polished, patent leather shoe. The cluttered space was filled with the calming scents of cedar and birch, while hidden speakers played 'Cavatina' from The Deer Hunter.

Barely visible in a dimly lit alcove, the brown loafer scraped against a chair leg as someone leant forward to apply more pressure on their blade. Clamping the handle in a vice-like grip, the tension he was feeling, peeled away with every slither that spilled from his deft cuts. A lucky gene pool and years of rugby had given our man forearms that could compete with the joists propping up his roof and at six foot five, it is fortunate that the beams created a tall archway that ran the entire length of the second floor.

His enjoyment of the tranquil music was cut short, when Bluetooth was interrupted by a deep ringtone coming over the wireless setup in the rafters. Treading on wood chips, he reached for his mobile and answered.

"Maddox here." Then a female voice with a strong Scottish brogue filled the room.

"Detective Inspector Maddox, this is D.C. Buchanan, I've been assigned to the funny girl case."

Melodic sounds of the highlands bounced off timber as she spoke, then Maddox dropped the pen knife into his trouser pocket, before speaking himself.

"And?"

Grace Buchanan had rehearsed her first conversation with Detective Inspector Jonathan Maddox over and over, but his one-word reply hadn't cropped up in any of the scenarios.

"Er... shall we meet, sir?"

Maddox glanced at his watch. "Are you at the station?"

"Yes sir."

He turned the length of basswood in his hand. The highly sought-after timber was venerated in the whittling fraternity, mainly for its soft carving qualities.

"How does your mother address you, Buchanan?"

Static hovered in the airwaves between phones and the constable relaxed a little.

"Er... Grace... sir."

The inspector was always fair with juniors but very firm. "Pick me up in half an hour, Constable, oh and Grace!"

"Yes sir." She smiled.

"Don't let me hear you refer to it as the funny girl case in future, will you?"

Grace frowned at the other end. "Absolutely s—"

The line went dead. She looked up at the front desk and called over, "Hey Sarge, where does Maddox live?"

Chapter 8

When the lovers arrived back on earth, they soon realised that it had begun to rain, and quite heavily. Earlier, the rustic roof light had inspired their passion but now, its drawbacks were clear, so after a quick smoke they headed for the cover of Cherry Tree Farm. The evening was still warm despite the downpour and a steamy mist clung to the tarmac as the couple marched toward the landmark heap of decaying manure that so revolted Erin. By the time they arrived, it was just a dark shape in the gloom but she knew it was there because of the stink while sidestepping it and avoiding the gate.

Protection from the weather and not being spotted

was Flynn's priority so he ducked under a rickety lean-to, with his girl in tow. Now he could get his bearings and formulate a plan. Two abandoned tractors seemed to stand guard over a moss-covered caravan that had long since collapsed under its own weight, its pale colour tinged green by elements that now tapped an irregular beat on its tin roof. In the darkness, as Erin wiped her sodden fringe with the back of a hand, it occurred to her that there was something out of place about the lighting at Cherry Tree Farm. State-of-the-art tungsten illuminated every recess and outbuilding surrounding the dilapidated farmhouse, yet nothing about this time capsule from the 1930s, complete with outside toilet, seemed to merit such a spectacular show.

Here and there in the muddy courtyard, sprigs of straw glinted under floodlight and an unusually large boot print filled with rancid rain water, before overflowing into another metre-long puddle and then the next closely spaced pool. More of the prints gathered around an open doorway on the side of the farmhouse and an orange glow from within had cast long shadows into the deep impressions. Perched on top of three granite steps, the substantial entrance offered a bird's-eye view of the stormy night, some of which was now being swept across flagstones, past the old-fashioned stoop, before settling on a massive pair of leather hiking boots.

Flynn shifted his weight onto his right leg, using Erin to balance as they crouched together underneath one of the tractors. His touch on the girl's arm gave her comfort in the shadows so she reached out for his hand, only to find her own damp skin instead. He was already halfway across the yard by the time she'd refocused on the night, spotting him splashing his way toward that warm glow shimmering through the darkness. Then, teeming rain stung her own shoulders as she too left their refuge and sprinted to join her boyfriend by the steps. Halfway there, her progress ended when she tripped in one of the huge footprints. Erin cried out as a knee shuddered painfully, giving way from under her, and silvery rhinestones twinkled in the dusk as they scattered from a sandal when it was ripped from her sprawling foot, sending the girl down with a violent thud.

Chapter 9

Grace thought that wipers on intermittent were enough for the present conditions. The earlier downpour had turned to drizzle as she cruised along the narrow cul-de-sac, negotiating any protruding wing mirrors. At the end, it became a horseshoe and an athletic-looking man sat there, on what appeared to be a sports hold-all. Kitted out in tracksuit garb, he waved a hefty arm at her and Grace wondered if he would actually get through the passenger door of her little Fiesta. Pulling the handbrake on, she got out to open the tailgate.

"Evening sir," she called over. Maddox threw the bag at her feet and got in the car.

Grace Buchanan kept herself fit and was extremely lithe from Taekwondo classes but she was actually considering climbing inside that giant hold-all to avoid this early confrontation with the inspector. Then, thinking better of it, she hurled the thing into the boot space and sat behind the wheel, ignoring the fact that the inspector's knees were wedged against the dash and his head touched the roof lining.

"Thank you, Constable." His tone was friendly enough, she thought.

Chapter 10

Erin's life didn't flash before her, just today's little adventure came to mind. It all began so well, with the romantic liaison in England's country garden. Now, covered in scratches and bruises, spread-eagled in mud, the trainee nurse suspected that she'd broken her ankle.

After a minute or so, she lifted her tearful face out of the slime. She was laying on a slight incline, so strained somewhat to raise her aching head enough to see. Through blurred vision and sweeping rain, an image assembled itself in the near distance. Erin's freckled brow furrowed and she took a sharp intake of breath. To her, it looked for all the world as if a headmistress from five decades ago was lifting an unruly student off their feet, by the throat.

Chapter 11

Starting the engine, Grace released the handbrake but had to scrape past his thigh in doing so.

"Sorry sir." She sounded nervous to Maddox but he found the Celtic timbre of her voice curiously attractive.

"No worries, Detective, just get me to the rugby club, will you? I'll point the way."

They set off for the training ground on the south side of town, which coincidentally, lay opposite the brand new hi-tech investigation centre.

"Forgive me sir, but is that a New Zealand accent I'm hearing?"

Maddox gestured to take the next left with his huge hand, and Grace couldn't help thinking that the man's thumb was probably wider than her own bony wrist.

"Very observant of you, Grace, it appears that we are both away from family."

She smiled at that and took the left turn.

"Rugby's in the blood then, sir?"

Maddox signalled to go straight on at the lights.

"Could say that, but tonight I train the juniors. Go left at the roundabout please," he prompted.

Grace slowed for traffic and thought to herself that she just might get on with Inspector Jonathan Maddox.

Chapter 12

Flynn didn't see his girl, or even think of her. Maybe if he had, his concern might have stirred some anger inside of him. As it turned out, any rage that he felt, was swamped by shock and terror. Above him and in those massive boots, a towering figure grinned at Flynn and drew something from him that he hadn't uttered in fifteen years. Wrapped in dribble, the word 'Mummy' issued from Flynn's gaping mouth, then the ogre reached down and lifted him clean off the floor. Freakishly long fingers meshed together under his chin and hoisted the lad four feet into the night air. The stricken young man considered himself to be reasonably brave but after glimpsing the abomination in the doorway, he only dared snatch a brief look at it from the corner of a squinting, rain-stung eye.

It was pissed off, but that wasn't the worst of it. Then as urine spread down Flynn's Levi's, the giantess put him under her arm as if he was a piece of rolled-up carpet. A few metres away, Erin felt like she was in a dream, she wanted to run but something wouldn't let her. She guessed it might be fear, although a fractured fibula didn't help matters. The palms of both hands were hot from shards of slate embedded in them and her skull ached like crazy. Although her view of the scene was hampered and part of it was in silhouette, logic had reasoned with her and it told the girl that the surreal pantomime being performed next to the farmhouse, had to be her beau in the grip of an eight-foot monster. She had to get out of sight, and fast. For a few seconds, Erin wondered if it was a myth that terror could paralyse a person. She'd witnessed the teacher from Hell shake her boyfriend as if it was taking out the rubbish and now Flynn was tucked absurdly under a grotesque armpit. The only thing for it, was to roll back to the refuge of the rusting tractor. She managed it without too much pain but her view of the yard was now compromised by the mouldy caravan. At least out of the rain, it would enable Erin to collect her thoughts. She replayed the haunting images again and analysed the disturbing details.

"Nobody wears tweed anymore, do they?" The girl screamed this into the night but no one heard her. "Tweed trilby! Give me a fucking break," she hissed angrily, at the farmhouse.

The skirt and tunic of check was strange but the alarming part, had to be the scale of the woman, if that's what it was? With hands like sofa cushions and, "Fuck me, the head on it!" she cried.

Not only was it oversized, but long as well, with elongated features that would frighten a policeman. Thick rubbery lips, contorted with rage above a masculine jawline that was cleft and long. Everything about the ogre was long. Limbs that wrapped around Erin's boyfriend were big-boned and sinewy but looked immensely strong, as did its lanky stockinged legs.

A little way past the distressed caravan, a floodlight appeared to flash at Erin. But she knew that it hadn't flashed; something had moved between her and it. She scrambled to her grazed knees and saw that the towering figure had changed position. Rods of slanting rain, picked out by a second floodlight, pelted the headmistress as she moved down the slope towards the lean-to, where Erin was cowering. Then, through some broken slats in the wooden shelter, she spotted a pair of hiking boots. They were gigantic and stood in a six-foot stance. Freakish legs made Erin think of rugby balls strapped to four-by-four with tan stockings hitched over them.

Listening to her own breathing, Erin watched as the monstrous footwear shuffled on gravel next to some machinery. Thinking that she needed a better angle, the traumatised girl placed her cheek against some cold boards. Water droplets fell into her eyes as they shook, so she rubbed them with a forearm. The stinging sensation didn't last but when her matted eyelashes sprung apart, her boyfriend's terrified face swung into view, through the narrow slit between the timbers. Gravity drew tear-laden mucus over his pale eyebrows and Erin put a trembling finger to her lips in reassurance. The stricken boy didn't see her, and with a broken heart, she knew it, as an eerie stillness enveloped the air around her, leaving just the slow *tap... tap* of rainfall on the caravan, to punctuate the silence.

Then it shattered. Erin jumped out of her goose-pimpled skin at the sudden screech of scraping metal and groaning hinges, followed by the mechanical clunk of a lever being thrown. She felt her knees and thighs vibrate as some kind of motor exploded into life and the pungent smell of petrol fumes was overpowering as the atmosphere inside her hideout became unbearable. The industrial clattering noises echoing through the partition seemed not only violent in their ferocity, but strangely familiar. Something about it set alarm bells ringing for Erin but she couldn't quite place what. It troubled her, like a memory does or déjà vu. In her mind's eye, she saw her father's truck, then a black and white image of him came to her. The letters on his Hilux were small but just legible. 'BEN SUMMERS - TREE SURGEON.'

It hit her like a bus.

"A fucking tree shredder."

She mouthed it silently, then collapsed back onto the damp floor. This lower perspective gave Erin her first sight of the machine. Then it was obscured by the hideous profile of the mad woman. Erin swallowed as the shrieking of serrated blades rose higher in her ears and for a glorious moment she hoped that the contraption had jammed. Sadly, and with expanding horror, she realised that the high-pitched whining came from her sweetheart.

The ghastly vision in farmers' tweed had unceremoniously stuffed the helpless rave organiser feet first into the hopper of the Mighty Mac Shredder/Chipper. At the heart of the Mighty Mac, according to its manufacturer, is the shredding chamber or hammer mill. This houses twenty-four free-swinging hammers that shred, tear, beat and grind material until it is small enough to pass through the grid at the discharge end of the machine. As Flynn disappeared into the giant funnel, his torso shook to the rhythm of the cutters. Fortunately, the shock had already killed him.

Erin's tears streamed as Flynn's dead face bumped

over a rusty lip on the yellow hopper, smashing his front teeth against it and flicking a shiny white incisor onto the ground in front of her. Rolling over twice, it settled next to a rather stiff and unhealthy-looking rat. In the darkness, the tooth appeared to glow, and Erin sobbed for her lover. It was so clean! Then she noticed the lack of blood at the entrance to the funnel. That was reserved for the business end of the apparatus, where shredded leather covered in a pink mush was being propelled onto the concrete via a narrow metal chute, quickly followed by a mixture of denim, bone and flesh. This concoction was a relatively dry mix but the final pile spat out was much larger and wetter. With a thick torrent of congealed blood, it gushed as if a tap had been opened. Night time gave it the appearance of hot tar with the same consistency, and there was a lot of it, all running downhill.

One of Erin's worst nightmares would be paddling in a loved one's blood, so she took a deep breath and felt her way along the dark space, aiming for a flickering lamp at the farm's perimeter. Its triangle of diffused light shone down on something that seemed to call out through the mist to the girl, forcing a nervous laugh and wry smile. Erin never thought, in a million years, that she'd be glad to see that septic heap of straw again, but there it was, in all its majesty, not fifty metres away. Adrenaline pumping through her had a strange effect really. She felt apprehensive, but exhilarated at the prospect of those beautiful gates and escape, so placing a hand on a wooden upright, Erin pulled herself up.

"Fuck!" she whispered. Had she banged a ceiling rafter?

"Christ!" Probably a nail or rusty spike! She tapped the screen on her phone and aimed upwards. It certainly wasn't a nail though. Here WAS her worst nightmare. Erin cried out in terror but couldn't recoil because on the other end of an S hook that was embedded in her temple, was the most unimaginable individual on God's earth.

Theatrical torch light falling on those exaggerated cheekbones, didn't exactly promote film-star looks, and the thing stooping over Erin, seemed to bask in its own scare value. Through galvanised springs in a metal bed frame propped up against the wooden slats, giant red lips displayed equine standard molars and manic eyes delivered a knowing expression that said, "Gotcha." Then, in a macabre twist, headmistress whispered the word, "BOO!!"

In her haste to snare the prey, Violet Thorndyke unintentionally ripped the butcher's hook from the relatively thin skin covering Erin's skull, just above her ear. The pain was excruciating but short-lived and the girl's vision had become pixelated, like a computer screen on the blink. To Erin, it felt like she'd been in that Godforsaken shed forever, so the relief of clearing its enclosure brought more tears and whimpers as she exited its claustrophobic walls. She didn't know if she was ducking from rafters or freaks, but didn't care, and as in every bad dream, terror was chasing her. Then, just as in her sleep, it caught her.

Chapter 13

It was still tipping down when Punk Girl eventually came out of the shop. Dominic trailed his quarry across cobblestones but this time, he followed as she entered a fashionable boutique. Thorndyke made a habit of stalking lone females. If he spied an unaccompanied lady on the opposite side of the street, for instance, he would immediately stride through any traffic to get behind her, even if she was travelling in a different direction. The thrill it gave him was multiplied by a hundred if she actually glanced over her shoulder at the beast, and if the poor woman picked up her speed, noticeably panicked, then he'd be nearly hysterical with joy.

Out of the rain and umbrella down, he pretended to browse, while ogling the girl. She'd lingered at some cotton dresses just inside and as she ran a pale finger along the chrome rail, Dominic felt himself blush. Then, she snatched a bright one from its hanger and carried it to the counter.

The pervert watched from afar as the sales girl nodded and smiled to her, then Hallelujah, he couldn't believe his luck when Punk Girl pulled back the curtain on a changing booth. He did well to control himself as the bell dinged behind him but it was just the wind blowing the door open. Closing it, he casually made his way to the curtains.

Tilly will assume that I'm hubby! his inflated ego joked as he passed the shop girl and not only could the madman smell his target's perfume, he was sure he heard the twang of her bra.

"Dreamland, baby," he whispered to the curtains, then his phone rang.

The young lady at the cash register wasn't called Tilly, her name was Jess and she'd been trained to observe customers while pretending to be occupied.

All of her attention was concentrated on a tall man wearing a St. Gwendoline girl's school blazer that appeared to be four sizes too small and which, he must have acquired at Sue Ryder. She was convinced that the strange man wasn't with the trendy young lady trying the dress on and had become increasingly concerned with his behaviour. Now, the weirdo was talking into a mobile phone and at the same time, tweaking his left nipple through a T-shirt. Not only was it very inappropriate, he was doing it with much gusto.

Chapter 14

Driving to the county's main rugby centre, took Maddox and his new sidekick through some of the historical parts of town. Having lived here for more than a decade, he felt qualified to give a short tour of his beloved Bury St. Edmunds and showed her the thirteenth-century monks' abbey, informing the constable that centuries ago, barons of England met there to create the charter that would eventually become the Magna Carta. Grace politely feigned interest, resisting a yawn, and hoped that the sports ground was nearby. As it turned out, they weren't far at all.

Turning off the ignition, Grace looked sideways at her new boss as he spoke. "What do you know about the case then constable?"

She twisted in her seat. "Not much, sir, but I'll go over it tonight." Then, winding her window down she asked, "Is it true that a girl escaped, sir?" Maddox handed her a folder.

"Yes, and that young woman is our only lead. Here, go through this and we'll get together in the morning." He put a hand on the door to get out.

"Sir… you said something earlier!"

He hesitated. "What's on your mind, Constable?"

Now, she was hesitant. "About the joke, sir?"

He got out and closed the door. Grace watched in her rear-view as he retrieved the hold-all and came around to her side. The suspense was killing her and Maddox had to crouch down to look her in the eye.

"Read it yourself, Grace, I could do with some fresh eyes on this one."

She sat in her little car while he strode off with the massive bag on his massive shoulders, and decided that she really needed a drink.

Chapter 15

Dominic's disappointment was measurable and his erection died in an instant.

Only one person had his number or was remotely interested in knowing it. He hit the button.

"Hello Auntie." His voice was timid.

"Dominic?" He detested her deep nasal tones.

"Yes, Aunt Violet." He was flaccid now, and crestfallen. His aunt was speaking.

"Forget about any skirt you're perving over, I've got one."

Dominic's cock twitched. "Have you auntie… is she red?"

Violet cranked it up some more. "Oh yes, needy nephew, and is she ever to your taste!"

When Dominic spoke, an excited shakiness affected his words.

"And Pointy's, Auntie Violet?"

"Just get over here, Dominic."

This was too much for the little fucker and he soiled himself.

Chapter 16

Half a bottle of red later, her boots laying on the kitchen floor where she'd kicked them, and Grace had got nowhere with the case notes. The most intriguing aspect had to be their witness, Julia Bennet. She'd had a run-in with an undesirable in a car park of the West Suffolk hospital. After having her broken arm reset, she was attacked while getting into her car. Grace started to write a few questions down for Miss Bennet but the day had finally beaten her and she drifted off, curled up on the sofa, in her underwear.

Wine generally caused Grace to dream and it was the same one on every occasion. She had revisited the story a thousand times, but tonight, the last scene was different. The street she had been chased down for the last few years, changed, turning into a dead end or a cul-de-sac, and the pale hand on her shoulder that she could never identify, inexplicably belonged to a naked Jonathan Maddox.

Chapter 17

Before Dominic travelled back to Cherry Trees, he walked across town with Punk Girl. Maybe 'with' is stretching the point slightly. He was mindful to stay at least twenty paces behind her, all the way to a picturesque cottage near the cricket ground in Homefarm Lane. The cocky little waster imagined that he looked quite the part as he sashayed along on the balls of his feet, not once letting a heel strike the pavement, and totally ignorant of strangers giggling at the comical but harmless buffoon in the blue and gold blazer. They'd got the comical bit right and as Dominic sat on a bench at a rural bus stop, he rubbed his prominent knees energetically at today's good fortune. His little punk dish actually stopped and went through a five-bar gate at Dairy Cottage, the small pink dwelling that he'd admired on every bus journey, to and from Cherry Tree Farm, since he was ten years old.

Twenty minutes later, a number 42 dropped him off, on the other side of the first village out of town, then carried on to Wepstead and further. Dominic's home was about a mile away if he used the old Birdcage Walk to get there, so off he set. Not many people knew about the overgrown cut through that dissected Cooper's Farm, and Dominic treated it as his own personal rat run, scurrying under twisted blackthorn and creeping elderberry that vied for space above him. It didn't leave much room for light to get inside the leafy tunnel, but that didn't worry him at all, after spending so many years hiding from Aunt Violet and that temper of hers.

When he finally tiptoed out of the end of the prickly passage, the imposing rear facade of Cherry Tree's farmhouse dominated the moonlit skyline. Birdcage Walk had brought Rat Boy to the back entrance of his aunt's farm. His first instinct, was to look up at a top-floor window. It was in shadow, but he recognised the familiar form of a rosy-cheeked rag doll, with ponytails. This was the tried and tested signal to him, that the coast was clear.

A pair of black Wellington boots with the tops rolled down greeted him when he reached the steps and Violet was waiting. Then, a roll of bin sacks landed at his feet and Dominic cringed at her abrasive words. The deformed voice box of the aberration coupled with a substantial nasal cavity created a baritone sound as if projected through a very tinny loud hailer, and it grated heavily on Dominic's already fragile disposition.

"There's rubbish on the slab, Dominic, you'll need a shovel." She didn't wait for an answer and slammed the door.

Tools and agricultural equipment were stored in the big barn. So he trudged over with jeans tucked into wellies and unhooked its double doors. Their sheer weight allowed them to swing open, revealing a cavernous interior as dark as a cave and with enough room to accommodate any combine harvester. Unsurprisingly, judging by the surrounding fields, there was no combine. Parked just inside, and dwarfed by the huge space, stood Aunt Violet's Morris Traveller. The classic green car had to be kept spotlessly polished, even though she hardly ever ventured out in the thing, and Dominic took his valeting duties very seriously. Grabbing a brush and spade, he headed for the concrete slab area.

Violet Thorndyke tolerated her nephew and his illegal urges to a degree, but could not and would not abide the lowlife's obsession with pornography. Her fierce hatred of it, had more to do with envy than some moral code, and it often culminated in her tantrum and his pain. Now, in the fading light, Dominic felt a surge of anger. On the deck before the deluded idiot, under a yellow chute from Auntie's shredder, appeared to be his collection of adult magazines and paraphernalia. He thought he recognised one well-thumbed page laying on top of the pile and a narrow strip seemed to show a familiar triangle of flesh. The bridge of a nose and a rather lifelike eyeball stared back at him in the twilight, so

Dominic picked it up and lifted the floppy material closer to his own face.

Behind a crack in some curtains, Violet Thorndyke watched her weak nephew vomit his lunch over the remains of Flynn Bailey and being a considerate old soul, she described in great detail everything she saw to her pretty guest, who was indeed, the epitome of a captive audience.

Chapter 18

County court in Suffolk was held at Shire Hall in Raingate Street, opposite the police station, and the grand building looked from a period that Inspector Maddox might appreciate. So as Grace was buzzed through the front desk, she prayed to any saint listening, that they might grant her some cultural mercy. As it turned out, Maddox was in no mood for tourism today and they quickly left in his Audi. On her lap as they drove, was the blue folder he'd given her the night before. She broke the ice.

"Sir… can I ask you something? The girl who escaped. What happened there?"

He was curt. "You'll find out in ten minutes!"

"Oh… OK… I mean, great, sir."

He laughed out loud. "Have you had breakfast, Constable?"

"I don't really do breakfast, sir."

"No worries, Grace, we'll get this done and grab a coffee."

Five minutes later, Maddox was looking for a parking space. Mews Flats, it seemed to Grace, were the new-build sensation in the old town and the inspector was soon ringing the bell of a swish-looking apartment on the ground floor. The glossy black door opened and a young woman stood there. She was a redhead and her left arm was in plaster.

At that moment, Grace's training came to the fore and Maddox thought she displayed an impressive pair of bollocks. She had obviously read the notes and knew the girl's name when she introduced herself. Inside the flat, the detectives got their coffee sooner than they expected and Maddox insisted that Buchanan lead the interview. Grace grabbed the opportunity and carefully nudged the conversation in the right direction.

"In your own time, Julia. What happened in the car park?"

The woman cleared her throat. "I was getting my keys out... I had an idea that there was someone behind me but it all happened so quickly. He said... 'Are you OK?' and I started to say I was alright." Miss Bennett wiped her eyes. "Then he put a hand over my mouth and... I... well I told the police woman what happened."

Grace put a hand on her arm.

"Thanks Julia, if you can repeat it to me, that would be enormously helpful." Maddox was impressed.

"Well, my legs went and he must of put me in his car, one of those old ones with wood, and it was definitely green."

"Carry on, Julia." Grace thought she was a good witness and waited patiently while she adjusted her sling.

"I guess he thought I was out of it. Your colleague told me that the man had misjudged the drug dose on the cloth. I could hear him telling a joke and I thought I was dreaming. It reminded me of old music hall stuff when he put a gravelly voice on."

Grace sipped her coffee. "A joke?"

Miss Bennett was in full flow now.

"Yeah, a joke. He leaned across me to get my seat belt. I could smell his breath." She touched her nose. "I'm not good at jokes."

"Don't worry, Julia, just tell me!"

Julia continued. "He said… 'I went to the doctor.'" She scratched the top of her broken arm. "Then he clicked my seat belt and shouted in my ear… 'Doctor, I've broken my arm in two places!' But I was awake! And he started the engine."

Julia tightened her grip on Grace's arm.

"He was laughing like a mad man, but still had a punchline, I think it was… The doctor replied, 'Well don't go out then!'" Miss Bennett started to cry. "That was when I opened the door, he hadn't secured my seat belt and I ran to A&E."

Grace smiled compassionately at the girl. "Thank you, Julia, that was brilliant."

Maddox was finishing his coffee, which Grace took as a signal so she put her cup down and asked Julia if she'd seen the man's face. She said that he was always behind her and she was too scared to look anyway, because she sensed there was something terribly wrong about him. Maddox thanked Miss Bennett and they walked to the front entrance. Grace had got as far as the porchway when Julia called out to her.

"Miss Buchanan, there WAS something, I suppose."

"Anything could help, Miss Bennett," said the Constable.

"Well, when he came up behind me, there was a reflection."

Grace's teeth were itching. "Yes?"

"His coat, it made me think of my friend when we were growing up, she went to St. Gwendoline's Girls' School and that was her blazer."

Chapter 19

A behavioural science profiler might class both Thorndykes as monsters, but neither of the inbreds had acquired a taste for human meat... yet. Violet was reasonably content with hotpots that she left on the stove during the week, whereas her nephew fed his spindly frame with a never-ending supply of pre-packed sandwiches, all of which accidentally fell into his basket when grocery shopping with his elderly service users. He used to eat Violet's home-cooked fare until one day, through a half-closed door, he saw his aunt shaving her own toenails over a plate of stew, as if it were parmesan. There were two plates and Dominic guessed that he was destined for the surprise treat.

He was devouring some sandwiches now, tuna and cucumber in wholemeal, while his aunt checked that their guest was comfortable in the back parlour. On her return he flinched at the sound of the thumb latch, shrinking in his seat as she closed the old-fashioned door behind him.

"I saw you perving," she droned, poking an accusing finger in his face. When she lowered her skeletal bulk onto a Windsor-back chair, her stockinged knees looked down on a filthy plank of red oak that served as some sort of table and she was still a foot taller than her standing nephew. The finger in question, stretched almost the length of her nephew's forearm and in between the knuckles were thick bristles of black hair that Dominic always likened to the disgusting legs of a harvest spider.

Over the years, Violet's evil temper had become harder to control so Dr Sweetman had prescribed the strongest drugs at his disposal, and a regrettable side effect of these barbiturates was a skin colour more reminiscent of Coleman's mustard than her prisoner's milky porcelain. Dominic folded the food packet and tossed it onto the table.

"She's a ripe one, Auntie Violet."

His aunt was trying to clear her throat. Nostrils the size of egg cups came with their own set of problems, which Violet dealt with by stuffing a fat thumb into one orifice then emptying the other, with the use of her powerful lungs. Luckily for Dominic, and through gained experience he avoided a direct hit by quickly spreading his feet, and a phlegmy lump slapped the floorboard in front of him.

"You smelt her peach, dirty boy. I saw you!"

"Just a sniff, Auntie."

He was on Violet's hook now, so she reeled him in.

"Stand up and show me."

The ingrate put a bare foot in the snot as he rose and Violet's eyes rolled in that big old head.

"You idiot, come here."

He knew the routine and unbuttoned his trousers.

"Let's see if you need milking, dear nephew."

She got his penis out and proceeded to massage

the tip. His manhood was average in length and girth but looked very unimpressive in her fleshy digits as she teased him with a technique she'd perfected throughout his adolescence. Aunt Violet found the most efficient method of emptying him was by holding it between finger and thumb. Dominic was repulsed by her finely manicured nails, each one squared off, orange and considerably larger than a guitar plectrum. Then manipulating the end as if she were rolling a ball of Blu Tack, he would ejaculate with no trouble at all. Unfortunately, Violet had barely commenced the operation, when she felt the need to drag him by his member, over to the kitchen sink, where Dominic immediately spilt his seed over some grotty saucepans.

"You dirty little fucker," she sneered.

He didn't answer her. With eyes closed, gripping the sink with one hand and his cock in the other, Dominic heard Violet from another part of the house, even though she was right there next to him, wiping her sausage fingers on a fancy yellow cravat.

"Which one of your old bags is missing a scarf

then, you thieving little shit?"

He unfurled the silk from his neck and cleaned his helmet with it. Then decided to wash the dishes.

Chapter 20

Erin's choice of attire for a day's kidnapping now struck her as ill-advised while struggling against some rope that secured her feet and wrists to a milking stool. In the right context, her short summer dress would be fine, but in the dismal setting of Thorndyke's back room, its sheer fabric only served to fuel Erin's insecurities. The hem was still gathered at her belly from when that degenerate in the blazer had examined her, so she wriggled in a vain attempt at rearranging it.

Shutters on the only window meant that her sole light source came from a blue LED on an electrical extension plug behind her. Its effect was eerie, but gave Erin the opportunity to study the parlour and not withstanding her obvious predicament, the space made her feel very uncomfortable. The only room she'd been in, besides this one, was the kitchen, and that was seen from the floor as she was dragged in by her hair. This had the same feel with its running theme of nicotine yellow and fifties sideboard, but the most unsettling thing for Erin was another item of furniture. This one seemed unusually bespoke, and constructed entirely from welded steel. She'd seen something similar in nursing college but that was what disturbed her, although she was sure that the contraption parked in a dark corner had very little to do with patient care. Whoever had designed the thing, knew exactly what they required but because Erin was a well-rounded, emotionally balanced member of society, she couldn't get her head around its primary function. Until she'd put herself in the minds of her host and hostess, then all became clear.

*

The deviant pair had created a harness for sex, by cannibalising the carcass of an antique wheelchair and welding a tubular steel frame to the armrests. The main purpose of the scaffolding was to accommodate six stainless steel stirrups and chrome chin support, complete with retaining straps. Erin's aching heart sank even lower when she'd worked out that the configuration of the spoon-shaped stirrups, in relation to the position of the chin brace, meant that for a person to enjoy the benefits of the apparatus, they would have to climb into it, doggy style.

Chapter 21

Coffee at Miss Bennett's was OK, but Grace's creamy mocha in the Butter Market, really hit the spot. Maddox had paid for two cups and then left her sitting outside Toppers, while he nipped across to Waterstones book shop. It was cool in the shady corner, where midday sun never quite reached the sandwich bar, so she was glad of her leather jacket.

When the inspector sat back down at the cast-iron table, Grace told him of her intention to chase up what she could find on the school blazer, and Maddox warned her that the girls' academy had closed years ago and was now a hotel. Then, sliding a glossy hardback between the coffee cups, he broke the news that she'd be walking back to the station on her own.

"I also want you to concentrate on this, Constable," he instructed her, turning some pages and using a sugar pot to keep them flat. She crossed her fingers that this wasn't another lesson on historical Suffolk and eyed his book. On the right-hand page, was a colour photograph of two classic automobiles and a green one had a wooden frame at its rear. Maddox spoke again.

"Stay with me on this, Grace. My father owned one in blue, so I know what we're looking for. You should be aware that this is the car. Miss Bennett's assailant drives a green Morris Traveller."

Chapter 22

Later that day

The operations room at the station was always a hub of activity and this afternoon was no different. It was buzzing when Grace saw her governor come in, so she poured a second coffee and headed over. She was keen to get him up to speed before the briefing.

"Evening sir," she said, offering the paper cup. While he sipped the hot drink, Grace took her chance. "Sir, a girl's gone missing, and maybe her boyfriend as well."

Maddox groaned. "That's what this is."

She tried to judge his mood. "Yes sir. It's early days but with the girl hiker's still gone and with the recent attack, everyone's up for this one." Grace got the impression that the inspector's mind was somewhere other than the investigation unit, so didn't push the issue and payed attention to the chief super.

Some of the greener ones in the room nudged each other when the chief suggested that a young couple seemed to have vanished while canoodling in the countryside. The girl's jacket was found in a makeshift camp by some kids and had been identified by the girl's mother. The other point that the chief super wanted to make, was that the boy's den wasn't far from Hungry Hill. This little gem drew more nudges, so Grace looked at Maddox. She caught him examining the buffed handle on a well-used pen knife, and never taking his eyes away, he informed her, "Hungry Hill, Grace, is the last known area in which our girl hikers were ever seen."

He pocketed the knife and as Grace followed him out. He asked if she'd got the names of the couple. She read the names and addresses from her notes and both of the detectives concluded that the overused adage that a book should never be judged by its cover, was indeed very true.

Chapter 23

One hundred and fifty years ago, Albert Thorndyke's father was touched by the family curse and though he didn't pass the physicality on to his son, he made sure that the boy paid in other ways. Then, when Albert got married, he had a daughter and she inherited the entire range of the curse's abominations. The birth not only took twelve hours, but also the last breath of her mother and when Albert set eyes on baby Violet, his wrath surpassed his father's, in ways that couldn't be imagined.

Now, at five in the morning, the very physical and malevolent proof of that lineage was lumbering up the yard, towards Cherry Tree farmhouse. Violet lived the life of a vampire in many respects. She could move around in the dark hours without fear of snoopy neighbours and get on with chores, like retrieving the free press from their post box. Near the top of the slope, she reached a gravel area, in what used to be a small flower garden, where some chickens were pecking at tiny stones. A couple of the hens knew better than to hang around when she was in the vicinity, so legged it for cover.

Breathing heavily, Violet read the headline and her utter disbelief unfolded like the creased pages of her newspaper. Ancestral fury, handed down over centuries, bubbled and seethed under the surface of her subconscious, then began to boil. Before it erupted, she got herself out of sight and into the safety of her kitchen.

Dominic half dozed under a duvet, languishing in his corrupt world of sadism when he heard the foghorn that was his aunt. Dithering was not an option, unless he fancied starting the day with a swollen ear lobe. Stepping gingerly down the back stairway, he daydreamed with irony that Aunt Violet had prepared him a sumptuous breakfast and he would be met by sunlight pouring into the kitchen, starbursting off cutlery, and a steaming pot of coffee. All surrounded by salvors of hot sausages and eggs next to dishes of fried tomatoes, toast and mushrooms.

The reality was depressing. Turning the corner on the bottom step, it was still night time. Violet's boots were caked in mud and she was seated with some keys on the lap of her checked skirt. Dominic followed her eyes to the table and the *Citizen* free paper. Its headline screamed at him as the keys ricocheted off his temple and Aunt Violet told him to, "READ IT."

He started to mumble the words.

"OUT LOUD," she ordered him.

He sat at the table and narrated the headline.

"MAN IN VINTAGE CAR ATTACKS WOMAN AT HOSPITAL."

Then he recounted the story.

"A YOUNG WOMAN FROM BURY ST. EDMUNDS HAS BEEN ACCOSTED BY A MAN,

WHO ATTEMPTED TO DRUG THE VICTIM AND PUT HER INTO HIS CAR, WHICH IS UNDERSTOOD TO BE A GREEN 1967 MORRIS TRAVELLER. POLICE ALSO SAY THAT THE MAN MISCALCULATED THE DOSAGE AND THAT THE YOUNG LADY HAD A LUCKY ESCAPE. THE ASSAILANT IS DESCRIBED AS WHITE, TALL WITH DARK HAIR AND WEARING A ST. GWENDOLINE GIRLS' SCHOOL BLAZER."

Dominic peered up at his aunt, who was standing over him. When she opened those bulbous lips, a globule from her nose dripped onto the newspaper with a smack.

"Hide the car, Nephew, then see to our guest."

Chapter 24

Meadows and pastures all over England in June and July were being beautified in readiness for auto shows of every description, and no more so than in rural East Anglia. 'Cars on the green' in Bardwell was one such event. Villagers and committee members organised the displays, refreshments and entertainment every year and ploughed the profits back into the next year's show. The inspector found some of the examples rather sad, with the exhibitors' wives reclined in deck chairs, busy knitting, and their husbands enjoying lunch from the car's picnic basket, while perched atmospherically on the running board.

The thing is, Maddox loved old vehicles. In New

Zealand, a relatively young civilisation where he grew up, a classic automobile was something like the 1974 Datsun Cherry, because it was the first car in the world to come with a radio as standard. The likelihood of that model being here was extremely remote, and anyway, he was after something else. It also seemed too much to expect the Morris Traveller to be here at the show. Nevertheless, if anybody knew of one locally, then Rob Mathews might. Rob had run the event since day one and had kept a ledger with every car exhibited on the green, all the way up to now.

By the time Maddox had tracked him down, the beer tent had sold out of ale and the sun was dipping behind a row of poplars.

"Great little car," Mathews called out from under a 1939 Austin 8.

"Try it now, darling!" he bellowed.

A woman in a summer dress turned the key and the old four-cylinder fired up.

"Don't think you've met the wife, have you Jonno? Karen, this is Jonathan Maddox, the copper."

They shook hands politely, while Mathews got to his feet and wiped his hands on a piece of rag.

"It's not been in our show, mate, but didn't old Thorndyke have one? You know, the old git at Cherry Tree Farm. His was green as well."

Chapter 25

For a wee lass brought up in Edinburgh, life out in the sticks seemed positively utopian. The landscape couldn't be more different from the backdrop that moulded and influenced Grace's early years. Here in the leafy lane, sycamore replaced cathedral-scale monoliths and decaying bark impersonated Craigleith sandstone. She found the straw camp easily enough, but apart from a rather frazzled-looking pheasant, there was nothing much to write home about. Trudging the tarmac, Grace's phone told her that she was walking up Hungry Hill, back towards the outskirts of town, but she didn't need GPS for that. Lactic-filled calves and thighs like rocks confirmed this for the detective, in spades.

Ahead of Grace, on the brow of the infamous hill, she saw for the first time this afternoon something that might suggest human life. It was only a gate, but after two hours in paradise, she was desperate for anything. Behind the eight-foot-high steel, she was relieved to see an untidy farmyard. To her, it looked abandoned, but surely somebody around here would have seen the young lovers. A rusty padlock and chain had fused together to become one with the iron barricade, so she squeezed between the gate post and an immense pile of manure.

Grace made a mental note of some very large boot prints at the entrance, then lifting her gaze past an ugly group of cattle sheds on her right side, her eyes were immediately drawn towards the higher ground. Six sash windows on a three-storey house faced the young woman and for a fleeting moment she wished that Maddox was by her side. For, in only a matter of minutes, summer had been replaced by autumn on Hungry Hill and the granite block of a home faded as it hunkered down into the north-facing ridge, under an ominous-looking sky. A few metres from some steps at the side of the house, Grace paused at a sight to her left, that she struggled with initially. In an unkempt alpine garden with shingle and rocks, she came upon a montage that was disturbing, to say the least. Going by some orange and brown plumage, it appeared that a member of the poultry family, probably a chicken, had buried its head in the sand… or grit. The animal was up to its shoulders, and gravel had flowed back into the hole. More worryingly, its yellow feet were pointing skywards and the poor bird had squirted its entrails from its own backside.

Chapter 26

Violet always slept on the top floor of her house; she used the master bedroom because it possessed the only made-to-measure bathroom, furnished with a four-metre tub and toilet bowl on an eighteen-inch-high pedestal. Not only was Violet's Christian name one letter away from her job description, it was also the colour of her migraines and she was having one now. Dominic could hear her pneumatic snoring from the kitchen as he separated a pair of curtains under the sink. Quietly moving an archaic mincer to one side, he grabbed the can of oil that he needed. If he forgot to lubricate a cylinder and barrel in the parlour's door handle, it tended to creak and this reduced his chances of bursting into his playroom unannounced.

Today, the mechanism was as quiet as a mouse and the toad was able to frighten the living hell out of the wretched girl. Unfortunately for Erin, she was midway through untying a sports bra from around her ankles at that precise moment. Dominic didn't act with undue concern at Erin's disobedience, although he did mention his aunt's reaction if the girl didn't behave herself. Instead, he tugged on a cable directly above her head.

Years ago, a grand chandelier impressed visitors who were entertained in the parlour. Nowadays, the ceiling ring served as a support for Dominic's cable, in a block and tackle set-up. Erin shifted on the stool. During the last twelve hours, her main concern had been the quaint little sodomy machine in the corner, so she'd underestimated the do-it-yourself hoist, and now the looped end of it circled snugly around her throat. It occurred to Dominic that the ratchet could also do with oiling as he levered the handle to and fro. Through gritted teeth and wheezy breaths he addressed Erin. She couldn't believe her own ears as he spoke.

"Paddy's wife is just about to give birth!" he whispered.

The ingrate actually started to tell a joke and panted like he was moving a wardrobe.

"So he rushes her to the hospital!"

He continued while checking the cable, and his words were raspy. Erin was upright.

"'How dilated is she?' enquired the nurse."

Erin heard every absurd syllable, but was trying to keep her balance on the milking stool as the maniac delivered the punchline.

"Paddy replies, 'Ah Jasus, we're both over the fuck'n moon!'"

Erin Summers was absolutely incredulous as she swayed on tiptoes, then she heard a knock at the front door.

Chapter 27

Spits of rain fell in front of Grace as she backed away from the steps and waited for an answer. Behind her, were various items of agricultural machinery, including two antiquated tractors, so she knew where her escape routes lay. The door opened enough to allow someone to peek out, so Grace held up her badge. When it opened fully she was confronted by a nervous-looking male, who she guessed was about twenty-five-years old. While she gauged the man's demeanour and whether he was armed or not, Dominic did his own checks.

He surmised that the woman was a dyke because of her short hair and muscular thighs, but reckoned she might just turn after an evening strapped inside his sexy wheelchair. Grace spoke to him calmly. "Good evening sir, I'm Detective Buchanan from bury CID and we're asking local residents if they've noticed a young couple in the area."

Dominic shot a look over her shoulder at the shredder. "Not up here, Officer," he stuttered.

Grace had already made her mind up that he was a slippery one so she enquired about his name and why he was at the farm. While he answered, she scanned the shadows behind her, then turning back she heard a sound in the house like a chair being moved. "Who's with you, Mr Thorndyke?" she enquired, presenting an air of control.

"Oh, that's just the dog," he quickly replied.

Noticing a nervous twitch as he teased a yellow cravat at his neck, Grace asked him what was kept in the other buildings. The creature watched her jacket ride up over her waist as she pointed to the barn.

"Farming stuff and that," he replied, not giving too much away.

Grace was double curious now and she'd been polite enough. "Let's take a look, shall we, Mr Thorndyke?"

Dominic closed the door and led the way.

Chapter 28

Having not bothered with retying Erin's restraints, Dominic thought that he could leave her for a minute when he heard the front door knocker. The girl was still gagged with her own knickers after all this time but was too busy with the noose to loosen them. Then she heard the most beautiful sound in the world. The caller had said 'Detective', so in desperation she kicked the stool and it tipped onto its side, noisily. Erin regretted it immediately. Two things were specified when Old Man Thorndyke built the farmhouse. The first was a bespoke ensuite and the second was ten-feet-high rooms. Now, swinging from one of those ceilings, three feet above the floorboards, Erin's face turned blood red and she thought of her beloved Flynn.

Chapter 29

In the failing light, the magnificent pair of barn doors seemed to reach up to the star-filled sky forever, and as they swung towards her, Grace unholstered her Glock. The barn was pitch black and apart from a very grateful pigeon that glided from the hay loft and swooped a little too close for comfort, it appeared to be empty. She thanked Thorndyke and refastened the clip, but a nagging feeling that Grace couldn't shake made her peer upwards, past some wet tiles on an outside toilet and beyond. In the eves, she imagined something watching her, so studied the shadows and there it was. In a darkened window, two sunken eyes stared down and seemed to drill right through her own. Grace's heart missed a beat and Dominic caught a tantalising glimpse of flesh again as she laid a jumpy hand on the Glock, only to release it just as quickly when her own tired pupils fell onto the rosy cheeks and ponytail of a rather spooky rag doll.

Grace was positive that she'd be running into the strange Mr Thorndyke again someday and her teeth were itching big time as she made her way through that mud-caked straw, to the gates.

Dominic gave the bitch a respectful thumbs-up when she glanced back, then casually climbed the three steps. With one last look to make sure he was safe, he shouldered the oak panel as hard as he could, cracking the door against a sideboard and following it inside. Then, a not so cool Dominic threw himself at the parlour. Drowning in a sea of panic, he headbutted the frame as he floundered, grasping for anything to save his fall, after tripping on Aunt Violet's bare foot.

The door handle creaked terribly, but it was never going to alert Erin. If this were the movies, Dominic would have been greeted by a peaceful-looking woman, arms at her side and head lolling. Sadly for

Erin, it was much worse. The poor girl's right hand was blue and snagged between her chin and the cable. She had slipped back in the noose so that both ears were trapped under it and the loop had tightened on her jaw, so that a half-severed tongue lay against purple lips that had swollen and bled profusely onto her legs and feet. She appeared far from peaceful.

Dominic was sobbing. Largely for missed opportunities, and out of frustration, but mostly because of the monstrosity that now lifted him from the floorboards by his scruffy hair.

Chapter 30

When asked by the vicar of St. Mary's for the chosen name on her only daughter's christening, nineteen years before this gorgeous summer's morning, Janet Margaret didn't reply with the words 'Punk Girl' but the much more elegant Sophie Mae, after her own mother, and now Janet's first born was housesitting for her grandmother while she visited a sick friend in Cornwall. Dairy Cottage was listed and had a thatched gambrel roof with ornate pierced barge boards.

According to English heritage, it also boasted rusticated rendered quoins but for Nathan, Sophie's companion, it was all about the garden. Not to say he was green fingered though. Any contact Nathan had with horticulture was hanging on to the petrol tank of his Honda Enduro as it hurtled up a grassy bank at Wattisfield motocross. His open-faced crash hat sat on the breakfast bar with a pair of leather gauntlets, while the bike's stand gouged a small trench in some pea shingle under the porch.

Nathan himself, was enjoying a very rare treat for someone of his modest background. From an orange towel on the parched lawn, he had become mesmerised by his own rapidly drying footprints on a sun-scorched patio. Spread out on his belly in navy blue boxers, the loose cotton type, while letting the rays do their work on his torso, he switched his gaze from the water marks, to Grandma's swimming pool. It still rippled from his dive as Sophie watched him support his chin on tattooed knuckles, from a summer house. Eyes of green gazed back up the long garden to Granny's cottage, and she counted the days they'd been there. She'd arrived on Tuesday and Nathan joined her on Wednesday afternoon.

"Four days and the boy hadn't touched her," she said to herself, while getting up from a wicker settee.

Leaving the dappled shade of a bay tree beside the changing room, she released the straps of her one-piece, let it slip down to her hips and walked across the Indian sandstone circling the pool. Before she got to Nathan, she dipped a toe in the water and saw him turn onto his back. He hadn't even noticed her bare white breasts against the electric blue of her costume so she tugged the garment even further down her stomach.

Chapter 31

Van Morrison crooned his way through 'Coney Island' as the inspector headed back for his meeting with Buchanan. A red evening sun filled his windscreen and Maddox wondered what Karen Mathews looked like without that dress on. Rob's other half was a handsome athletic woman and very tall, just his type, so he put the window down and scrolled back through his memory to see her legs again. Their muscular calves hinted at a sporty background and he recalled a hockey-playing ex-girlfriend from his home town. She drifted across the bedroom of his mind as 'Van' worked his magic with 'Moondance', then turning it up from the steering wheel, he suddenly saw Grace. She wasn't what he usually went for, was she? Younger... slimmer... prettier... and next to him, naked! Jonathan Maddox felt a heat in his face that he hadn't experienced since middle school. Then, as pale imaginary fingers rested on his, he glimpsed a curve of flesh under her arm when she pulled his hand away from the wheel. A longing seemed to wash over the inspector as he gave some of himself away to the moment, allowing her to lead him somewhere that he wasn't quite sure about. Before they reached that place though, something whispered in his ear and he thought it might be decency, as with the coldness of leather, 'Moondance' dragged him back to the vivid crimson ribbon that stretched out ahead of his Audi.

Chapter 32

When Sophie poked a damp foot into the top of Nathan's shorts, he wasn't that surprised. Her presence had blocked out the sun breaking through his eyelids as she approached, and anyway, this had been on the cards for days now. Nathan Rhys considered himself to be a gentleman and thought it only polite to open his eyes. When he did, he was greeted by a goddess in a halo of shimmering haze. Both nipples were in relief and the raised profile of her flawless neck spoke to Nathan of sexual control and obedience. Reaching out, he hooked a finger in one of the straps and as he pulled it taught, Sophie helped him by stepping away slightly, letting the swimsuit fall gently to the grass.

The sun was Nathan's friend today and the silhouette was telling him that Sophie Mae was a woman who liked to keep herself au naturale, which he was a big fan of. It also whispered in his ear that he should take her in his arms and kiss the mound of flesh surrounding that butterfly in her navel, but the girl was gone. Sophie didn't need the sun to predict her future, her toes said everything. He wanted her, and the boy would get his way if he could catch her. Exiting his boxers she ran to the pool's edge and dived into the cooling water, but not to dampen her ardour. Enjoying the heat of the moment she exploded to the surface, sleeked her spikes back and waited for him.

The chase was everything to Nathan, as rather gracefully for a biker, he leapt to his feet and removed the shorts in a single stroke. Then he was beside her and she feared that the waters might boil. He kissed her, before she swam away on her back, making waves and teasing him with her small breasts.

Against the deep crimson of a Lilo, Sophie's pale

legs and buttocks were hypnotising for Nathan. Lazily floating towards the shallows on the inflatable, she swept a hand through the water as he stood, hands on hips, facing the deep end in anticipation of her arrival. Droplets of water glistened on her back as she drifted, and a curious thing entered Nathan's head; he thought of a cross channel, roll on, roll off ferry, and then she took him in her mouth.

Using his hands against the water to balance, Nathan closed his eyes and raised his face to the sun. Sophie was remarkably good at this, he thought to himself, opening them again and loving the sight of her arse cheeks bobbing to the rhythm of the waves. Pleasuring him was obviously important to her, so Nathan held fast and soaked it up. The soles of her feet were tinged pink and he watched them stroke, left and right as she too, steadied herself in the water, gripping his buttocks hard to anchor her.

He was ready now, so spinning her away on that Lilo, she arced full circle on the water until he could grab both ankles and pull her to him. Because of the moment and the pool and Sophie on her belly, he eased inside her like they had been together forever and she cried out for him. She was glad when he grasped underneath and found her knees, moving her in the water and using the inflatable to slide her back and forth on the biggest hard on he'd ever experienced. It had made it into Sophie's top five as well but the stiffness was also his undoing, because the view of her beautiful shape on the water slapping his groin was too much. So navigating her to the edge of the pool, where she gripped the side, Nathan held her thighs and as the Lilo washed away beneath them, he pounded those white cheeks and the lovers orgasmed together against the coolness of some pool tiles.

Chapter 33

Grace picked up chicken pasta salad and an orange juice from a one-stop before meeting Maddox at the station. She wasn't really enjoying the peri spices when he rocked up beside her, so pushed the plastic tray to the table edge, where it slipped over, into a litter bin.

Dropping a bag of doughnuts onto her papers, Maddox sat down and Grace noticed, not for the first time, that her boss didn't just sit in a chair, he attacked it, owned it. She took a doughnut.

"Fuck the rabbit food," she sighed and Maddox, who was facing her with legs akimbo, stuffed another sugary delight into his mouth.

"How'd you get on then, Grace?" He seemed in good spirits.

"Waste of time really, sir, what about you?" She waited while he finished another doughnut.

"Didn't find the car, but I might have something for you."

Grace took out her notebook as he wiped sugar from his lips.

"It seems that a local landowner had the same model in green. He's long gone now, but his family still own the farm, Cherry Trees, out on Hungry Hill."

Grace nearly choked on her doughnut.

Chapter 34

Violet always wore her hair up. She kept it in a bun, sporting a hat of some description at all times. Dominic thought her most ridiculous one was today's example. A splendid deerstalker designed for a much smaller head was perched on the bun and as with all of her hats, it was secured with a decorative pin.

When your common or garden variety serial killer needs to dispose of a human body, a type of saw will enter the equation somewhere along the line. Not for Aunt Violet though. She came out of the pantry wearing her best apron over a green tartan ensemble and wielding a magnificent cleaver with an eighteen-inch blade. More to the point, it boasted a depth of nine inches. That would easily cope with Erin's slight frame, which now lay prostrate and fully drained on the kitchen table.

Apart from her neck, the most demanding cut would be the femur, just above the knee. For the next one, Violet preferred a V shape above the pelvic bone. Two deep incisions at the navel, parallel with the ribcage, and that would separate the bulk of the body from the legs. Removing the arms at the shoulders would come next, then it was just a matter of the hands and feet.

Earlier on, once Dominic had recovered, he did as ordered and placed an old tin bath on the floor below Erin's swinging corpse. Then using some scissors, he undressed the body. Violet watched him get unnecessarily close as he drank in her odour, then saw him glance over at the contraption of sex in the corner.

"It seems a shame to waste it, don't you think, Auntie?"

Even Violet was taken aback at that little pearl. Not because of her delicate sensibilities, but after informing the brute of their time constraints, she explained that the noticeable onset of rigor mortis would probably mean them sharing meal times with Erin until she had rotted enough for them to remove her from it.

Finally, she showed Dominic where to nick an artery at the Achilles on both ankles. He didn't have the appetite for the butchery side of things, especially Violet style. Every deafening blow, every single slash and laceration were aimed at humanity and he'd already been on the end of it. She saw the blood draining from his face, so sent him to light a fire while she crudely dismembered the corpse. Erin's remains were destined for some pigs on Cooper's Farm, but her belongings and the stained block and tackle would have to be burnt.

Chapter 35

Reacting to information gathered at their meeting, the detectives took a wander up town. They'd received a call about the blazer so Maddox offered to show the constable a shortcut through Saint Mary's graveyard. Their destination was a charity shop near the centre so they walked in the abbey gardens and then along Abbey Gate Street. Maddox counted approximately ten watering holes on their journey and at the eleventh one, the Nutshell pub in the traverse, its lure of real ale on tap was too strong. Being the smallest genuine pub in England, they had to stay outside with the smokers and enjoy their drinks but Maddox didn't stand on ceremony. After his first sup, half a pint had disappeared and Grace was still people watching without touching hers.

She wasn't a great drinker while on duty. Not out of some need to adhere to the rules or anything, she just didn't enjoy alcohol while working a case. She found it hard to combine the two pleasures, as if she should personally suffer until the job was done. That meant not much sleep, grabbing a bite while on the move, and no time for relationships.

Maddox watched her through the bottom of his glass, while she sipped her Riesling.

"Fancy a refill, Grace?"

She rolled the glass between her palms. "Sir, why don't you have another, while I go see the old girl?"

The tavern's curved windows allowed Maddox to see inside and the landlord was busy finishing his crossword. Grace could virtually see the shop from the Nutshell so the inspector took her glass and made for the bar.

Five minutes later, a bell announced Grace's arrival inside the charity shop and a white-haired lady smiled at her from behind the counter. She showed the old dear her badge.

"Oh!" The pensioner sounded disappointed. "Sorry my love, I thought you were the records girl."

Grace looked unsure. "I did phone ahead, Mrs Cormack?"

"Yes, you're right my lovely, it's just that nowadays they have to check for rare vinyl, you know, collectables and such like. Everyone's a bloody expert these days!"

Grace smiled at that and gently reminded her about the blue and gold blazer.

"Of course, dear, the strange man in the funny jacket, I remembered him because he stole one of our scarves."

Grace stopped staring at a silver watch under the glass of the counter and looked up. "What colour was the scarf, Mrs Cormack?"

The old girl was on a roll now. "Yellow, definitely yellow with red tassels."

Grace wondered if she should book an appointment at the dentist.

Chapter 36

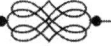

Sophie spent most of her teenage years bouncing between her parents' separate homes. Dad's flat in London and Mum's end-of-terrace in Horringer village. Situated west of town, the tiny hamlet was high on the National Trust's calendar, but blink as you drove through and you'd miss it.

She loved the Victorian land workers' cottage and her mother still lived there with her three dogs, all West Highland terriers. Recalling her free-spirited upbringing, Sophie snatched a memory down as it went by. A group of mum's women friends and herself were crowded around a birthing pool in the sitting room. Mum's best friend was kicking and screaming the house down and the pool burst. Sophie never dared mention this to her school mates but when she got to the Dog and Partridge, to meet Roxy and Jo for drinks, they would hear every erotic detail of Sophie's pool sex.

Chapter 37

'Diamonds are a girl's best friend' is how the song goes.

"Maybe it's time to update the lyrics," Nathan speculated to no one but himself.

But 'mobiles are a girl's best friend' didn't exactly roll off the tongue. Earlier on, after Sophie had left the cottage, her phone went off and he let it ring while zipping up his cargo pants. She'd left it in the summer house.

"A girl's gotta be connected."

He decided, while pushing his head though a cap-sleeve T-shirt. Casting his mind back to an hour ago, he saw Sophie, dripping water as she strode away from him and the pool. Amazonian woman on the catwalk would be the halting image he'd recall, later on that day. He'd watched her disappear through the conservatory, then swam to the edge, and followed her inside. They made love again, in the shower, and now he was alone once more and Sophie had gone out, leaving her mobile.

Chapter 38

Sergeant Grahame phoned Grace when she was on her way back to the pub; she took the call outside Poundland and he told her that a Morris Traveller was still registered at Cherry Tree Farm. Then, before crossing the taxi rank near the Nutshell public house, she saw Maddox sitting on his own, blue chinos spread, dark shirt tucked inside a thick oxblood belt and sleeves rolled past his elbow. Resisting any sense of guilt, the constable studied the inspector from a doorway. Before meeting him, Grace felt that she knew the man by reputation and after spending time with him, she'd grown to respect Detective Maddox. But there was more. She watched him through a blur of shoppers and drinkers, savouring his ale and joking with a girl collecting glasses. Then, sitting down to drink her wine, Grace realised that she really wanted to learn what that 'more' was.

Two flagons of beer passed overhead as they enjoyed some salty bar snacks but it was a different girl carrying them. She recognised Maddox.

"Zero beer, Jonno," she remarked, on seeing his glass. "You running a temperature, mate?"

To Grace, his easy smile seemed genuine.

"Gotta keep a clear head, Becki!" he countered. "By the way, this is Grace, my partner in crime."

She and Becki did the hello bits and then the tankards floated off into the crowd. Grace told him about the blazer and the call from the station while they finished the Bombay mix and later on, behind the wheel of his A6, on their way to Cherry Trees, Maddox would feel a little frustrated at her for leaving that tasty tit bit about the scarf till last.

Chapter 39

High above the avenue, branches of sycamore allow the odd tube of sunlight to permeate its patchwork of green and orange. Nature has created its own lampshade for Sophie's afternoon stroll, where butterfly leaves of yellow and red take off and land, some doing acrobatics as she marches a channel through summer's late carpet. With stilettos of gold, safely in her bag, the girl's pink running shoes kick their way along the quiet road where no vehicles have passed since she joined it at Fox and Pin lane.

Hankering after Nathan wasn't like Sophie at all, but she was glad of it now and daydreamed about the boy, between her legs. His hands all over her again, the strength of his thighs and the water caressing her calves. She felt it now, but it was just leaves and a flurry of them brushed an ankle as a silver convertible roared down the avenue, bringing Sophie rushing back to the summery lane.

By the time the last leaf had settled back onto the tarmac, the Porsche was just a tiny speck in the distance and its turbo growl had been replaced by the rattling eleven hundred of a Morris Traveller. Sophie knew about last summer's missing hikers, through her grandmother. So when a strange car pulled in at the curb, she was instantly on her guard. Her own reflection stared back at her from the passenger window, then the glass lowered and Sophie was relieved to see the polite young man from the boutique. He'd been so respectful on the phone to his aunt, while Sophie tried on a dress, and now he was offering her a lift.

Chapter 40

There were no circus leaves in St. Mary's cemetery. Only a mosaic of wet foliage suggested a way through the ancient tombs and clumps of giant elm painted everything in shade for Grace as she aimed for the gravestone-shaped sunlight at the end. Keeping her eye on the ever diminishing silhouette of the her boss, she shortened her stride on the slippery path before stopping to read a phone text.

MORNING CONSTABLE.

ADDRESS FOR YOU TO FOLLOW UP

MR TRAVIS BROWN

3 ANGEL LANE

B.S.E.

Ip33 5ax

ASSOCIATE OF MISSING MALE FLYNN BAILY? REGARDS SARGE

Grace looked towards the distant figure of Inspector Maddox. He seemed to be floating in a silvery haze that shimmered around him, and that was playing interesting tricks with the perspective. It appeared as though she could pick him up like a small doll, but it was all an illusion and she knew that he was too far away to hear her cries. The constable also knew that this couldn't wait, so she messaged him and headed for her car.

Chapter 41

Nathan checked the compression and kicked down on his Honda. The bike started first time as usual but he resisted an urge to gun it out of the entrance on Granny's perfect shingle. Inside the breast pocket of his leather jacket, Sophie's phone buzzed again so he opened up the throttle and threw the Enduro down the track.

He knew her route after she pointed it out earlier in the week, saying that the shortcut saved her a two-mile trek. Weaving between tightly planted spruce presented a decent challenge for him and the trail quickly became a narrow ribbon of compacted earth, where tree roots broke the surface here and there, creating hollows and ridges to be wary of. He relished their treacherous qualities and with delicate tweaks of his hand, he wound the twist grip on the handlebars and picked his way between the thick trunks slipping and grabbing with his back wheel. It wasn't too long before Nathan saw some tarmac cutting across his eyeline so he knocked the bike down a gear, dabbed the brakes and coasted towards it.

Chapter 42

The inspector got himself a coffee at the station and signed out one of the carbines. He generally went for a semi-automatic Heckler on a job like this, mainly because he could see how many rounds were left in its translucent magazine. Behind his desk, Maddox accessed the station's matrix and Thorndyke's skeletal features filled the screen. He had requested records on undesirables of a similar profile in Suffolk and found that Dominic was already on their radar for pestering females in the town. He'd been arrested and cautioned a couple of times but considered low risk. Maddox had heard that one before and wondered about the firearm Grace carried.

According to the authorities, Thorndyke was a support worker in the care industry and lived on his own, up at Cherry Trees. The farm was non-profitable since his father died, seven years earlier. Maddox already knew that it was in ruin, after speaking to Harry Cooper. Something else that the system flagged up was the Morris Traveller, registered to a Violet Thorndyke – deceased, but the nugget he was searching for came last. Two shotguns were registered at Cherry Trees.

Chapter 43

Angel Lane was situated in an upmarket part of town, close to a hotel of the same name. Next to this, stood a grand, three-storey brick building, very typical of the area. The old dispensary had seen out the Napoleonic wars, but now it had Travis Brown to contend with. His bedsit was at the top of a well-worn staircase that started at the front door and a curvaceous young girl sporting a grubby vest and bare feet led Grace to the landing. She introduced herself as 'Trav's girl', and it was probably his shirt that she was nearly wearing. Following her on the creaking boards, Grace paused halfway up to make a detailed inspection of the stair risers, after noticing that Mr Brown's girlfriend had chosen to go commando this afternoon.

Before entering the one-room flat, she imagined an unmade bed in a corner, with a scruffy unshaven male sprawled on it, probably watching 'Countdown' while rolling a spliff. She wasn't disappointed, even about the marijuana, but had more pressing matters to worry about than recreational drug use, so ignored the fat joint smouldering in an ashtray. He didn't get up or even acknowledge the detective but she'd dealt with his type a thousand times before and he'd already given her leverage, if she needed it, with the dodgy cigarette. Fran kicked the unlaced Vans on his feet.

"Visitor," she announced. Grace didn't profess to be perfect and noticed 'Deal or No Deal' on the television. That meant it was much later than she'd realised, so speeded up the process.

"Mr Brown, I need you to answer some questions for me, about your friend, Flynn Bailey."

He looked at her for the first time.

"Flynn... what's he done now?"

Brown didn't seem overly bothered and had

unravelled himself from the food-stained duvet, to stand up.

"He's a missing person."

The constable chided herself for underestimating Brown's size as he moved to the only window.

"Flynn's gone AWOL! Tell me something new, will ya?" he grunted, while his girl pulled on some knickers.

When Grace mentioned Erin's jacket, Fran piped up.

"He didn't take her as well, did he?"

She'd put her foot in it and Grace spotted Brown in a mirror over the sink, shaking his head and glaring at the stupid girl. With that, the constable seized her chance and retrieved the roach from the ashtray. She turned it in her fingers like a pencil, while focusing on Brown's expression.

"I need your co-operation on this, Travis, and fast!" she barked.

His face said everything so Grace sat down on a rather large and professional-looking speaker.

"The jacket!" he enquired. "On Hungry Hill, was it?"

She nodded, and later, when he'd told her about the rave and after Grace had left, he relit the cannabis and shared it with his girlfriend.

Chapter 44

Sophie stooped at the window and smiled to the driver.

"Hello again," she said.

"Hey," Dominic called out. "I'm going into town, if you'd like a ride?" He was on his best behaviour.

The car's interior seemed very cramped once she was inside, reeking of old leather and saddle soap. Sophie assumed it had value, because someone had taken the time to protect her seat with an inco pad. A second odour that hung in the atmosphere stung the inside of her nostrils, but she couldn't discern it from another strong smell, the overriding stench of stale piss.

Shutting her door, she felt the window lever dig into her side and wondered if she should be accepting a lift from a virtual stranger. When he leant over to fasten her seat belt, Sophie politely declined his help and thought about asking him to let her out at the next corner, then she told herself to get a grip and anyway, the man was already steering towards a bus stop. Thorndyke's vehicle might be half a century old, but it had a damn good turning circle and before Sophie could grab the door handle, he had wrenched the wheel round and they were heading back the way they came.

"Hey, what are you doing?" she demanded.

Dominic had a slight overbite and it made him sound curiously feminine when he spoke.

"No worries, Sophie, the road's closed," he told her.

Now she was really spooked.

"How do you know my name?" she asked him and her own voice cracked.

Shooting her an irritated look, Dominic started to answer but stopped, when in Sophie's peripheral vision, an unnaturally large and bony hand reached out to her from the back seat. With the span of a tea tray and nails weirdly filed to perfection, it occurred to Sophie that it belonged to a female.

In that moment, which couldn't have lasted more than two seconds, Sophie's imagination ran riot as another giant hand grappled at her forehead. Hairy fingers like massive Frankfurters touched Sophie's face and they held some sort of cloth, then she caught sight of their grotesque owner. A caricature of ugliness filled the whole space above the front seats and the monster's homicidal grin revealed huge molars and bleeding gums, with gaps that you'd have to pick using a chopstick. She retched at its hot, putrid breath and Neanderthal brow, then Sophie remembered the inco pad as she simultaneously lost control of both bowel and bladder. That was the last thing she thought of as her nose was smothered and the world faded behind heavy eyelids.

Chapter 45

At first, Nathan thought he was seeing things when a vintage car trundled past with Sophie in the front seat. He was puzzled because it was travelling in the wrong direction, but more alarmed by the person in the back of the vehicle.

Standing on a foot rest, he pumped hard on the back brake with his other boot and steered into the skid. This brought the bike under control, cutting a shallow trench into the gravel and spitting a shower of stones at the little green car. Nathan watched as it drove away from him and when they were at a reasonable distance, he set after them. Cruising down the avenue, he tried to get his head around the situation. The girl with whom he'd just had fantastic sex in a tiny piece of paradise, was up ahead and being held against her will. He'd seen at least two strangers in the vehicle, one man driving and a second person behind Sophie.

Nathan could only work on the information his eyes gave him but the images were confusing. The hand that held his girlfriend was absurdly large and seemed to belong to someone in a Halloween mask and wearing a Harris tweed hunting hat, complete with feather. Computing these details as fast as possible, Nathan wondered where the hell they were going and how he could save her. Then they broke cover of the forest and were in a landscape of flat fields and big skies.

Chapter 46

Everything that Grace said to Maddox about the lowlife Travis Brown and his friend Flynn Bailey, the inspector already knew, apart from the rave story. They sat in his office drinking coffee while he brought her up to date on Cherry Trees and both agreed on paying the farm a visit later that night. Before they left, Grace remembered that she'd heard a dog in the house after Maddox had mentioned Thorndyke's late aunt, then the detectives called in at the armoury for a couple of bulletproof vests and the inspector's carbine.

A luminous glow bounced off the Audi's bonnet as Maddox negotiated a series of bends that led him into Suffolk's countryside. After that, the road out of town stayed straight for a good mile, before banking left, then its urban lighting ran out. Neither Grace nor the inspector were in a particular hurry. Aided by the darkness they could approach the farmhouse and search the outbuildings uninterrupted, before confronting Dominic Thorndyke.

Chapter 47

With Sophie's comatose weight slung over her shoulder, Violet followed her nephew through their kitchen and into the parlour. Ten minutes later, she left the back room and closed the door.

Five minutes after that, it opened again and Dominic came out carrying Sophie's shoes and clothes.

A vicious gale was blowing across Cooper's field when he got to the stables and threw them onto a fire. It was still smouldering from the previous day but he doused it in petrol anyway. Then with hood up and hands in pockets he watched flames lick at the oil drum's rim and her things disintegrate. Violet spied on her repugnant nephew from the kitchen window while she filled a saucepan of potatoes at the sink. Kidnap and murder it seemed, gave one a hearty appetite, so sausage and mash were on tonight's menu.

Chapter 48

While the nutty Thorndykes went about their daily tasks, Sophie regained consciousness. Blinking away sleep from tired eyes, it dawned on the girl that she was staring at an antique serpentine sideboard. In the subdued light, dozens of monochrome faces studied her from the highly polished surface, where silver and gilt frames jostled for position to exhibit the ugliest portrait. She recognised one of the group and then remembered the little green car.

With heart racing, Sophie wanted to check her surroundings but couldn't turn her head. Panic was not the only thing to stifle the terrified girl's movements. She felt cold steel under her chin and something looped over her skull, to hold it there. Then she worked out that both arms and legs were restrained. This realisation worsened her feelings of vulnerability and imprisonment but there was another thing. From behind Sophie, a light source of some kind cast an electric blue tint onto every object in her plane of vision. Forcing herself to squint at a photo, she saw her own shape picked out by the blue sheen and reflected back. So, with eyeballs straining, the helpless young woman glared at the image until it came into focus and with utter dismay she recognised her own naked form framed in gold. More coldness underneath the girl touched her belly and shins, then Sophie knew that she was trapped inside a chamber of torture, kneeling on all fours.

Chapter 49

After hiding his motorbike behind a hedge, Nathan sat in the dark, opposite an iron gate through which the Morris Traveller had disappeared. A whole hour passed by, plus the contents of a hip flask, before he'd built up enough courage to get to his feet and approach the farmhouse. While drinking, he'd seen the driver come out and start a fire, but now, Nathan was sure that both of Sophie's abductors were inside the dimly lit house.

The only sign of life, was a rectangle of light cast onto the yard, from a ground-floor window.

Nathan guessed it was the kitchen and sprinted across gravel to get there. Crouching against the stone wall, he held his breath and listened for what seemed an age. The sound he heard, was his own heart, then the silence was broken by the clatter of saucepans. Gripping the window sill, he dared to raise his head and steal a look through some curtains. The ill-fitting material gave no privacy at all, so Nathan had a good view into the room and at one of the occupants. He couldn't see Sophie, but the car's driver sat at a table, sideways on to the window. He had his back to a door that was on Nathan's left, so the next objective was to rush the kitchen and surprise the wanker.

Nathan was confident of overpowering the individual lurking there, but unsure about the freak that he saw earlier. Watching it carry Sophie up the steps when they arrived, his girl had looked like a baby in a mother's arms. If the mother in question was ugly as sin and slung the pitiful thing over her shoulder, head first. Before crashing through the door, Nathan hesitated at a scraping sound behind him and turned to look.

What happened next, was astonishing, and it caused Nathan to have a memory flashback of something that made an impression on him when he was just eleven years old. His father was watching the boxing on pay-per-view and Nathan sat on the floor between his slippered feet. The cruiserweight Evander Holyfield had moved up a division to heavyweight and tonight was his first defence of an American title. The fight didn't last long because in the second round, Holyfield, who was destined to become undisputed heavyweight champion of the world, hit his opponent Adilson Rodrigues, with a right hook more akin to a sledgehammer.

The amazing thing, was the impact that the punch had on his adversary. It stunned Rodrigues so effectively, that his left knee shot up towards his chest in an involuntary spasm, before he keeled over onto the canvas, unconscious.

Nathan's own leg went into jerky spasm, when Violet pushed a shiny hat pin through his left eye and out the back of the socket. It must have pierced the same area of brain that Rodrigues suffered trauma to, because Nathan suddenly performed an ungainly Irish jig, right there in the darkness.

Thorndyke had jabbed the thing so hard that when it ricocheted off the inside of Nathan's skull, it bent the end. Now the steel pin had become a hook and as he fell back onto the concrete floor, Violet was left standing there with an eyeball lollypop. Nathan's good eye watched her in mid-collapse but he didn't register the monster because he'd already stopped breathing.

Chapter 50

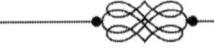

Maddox wasn't surprised when they came across the Morris Traveller. Once Grace and himself were in the farm's compound, he dropped the tailgate on an antiquated heavy goods lorry parked behind the big barn and climbed in. The old wagon had been converted into a horse box years before and now it could sleep two grooms as well. With huge springs attached to the trailer, the back door swung down and acted as a ramp so that Thorndyke could hide the infamous car until needed.

Before they exited the box, Maddox flipped the bonnet on the Morris and removed its distributor cap, then threw it over a fence. Grace waited outside, then led the inspector to the barn's great doors and while he tugged on a pair of iron rings, she peered up at the rag doll in the window. It still gave her the chills and gnawed at something in the back of her mind but whatever it was, she couldn't bring it to the front.

Inside the chasm-like space that could probably accommodate the entire farmhouse, Grace noticed something that she hadn't spotted on her first visit. In her torch's spotlight was a carriage that wouldn't have looked out of place on the film set of Mad Max. What got her hackles up though, were its dimensions. Maddox was curious as well and as he examined the wheels close up, she got a handle on the scale of the thing from further away. He gestured to her to come over and as she approached, she realised that, once upon a time, the wheels had supported a horse-drawn cart.

Nowadays the six spoked hoops took the weight of a colossal Heath Robinson type wheelchair and Grace hoped with irony, that she would never run into the person that the chair was created for. While she calculated the possible size of the user, Maddox did his own arithmetic and she watched him climb up the frame and get onto the wooden seat. He sat there, swinging his brogues back and forth like a big kid but a whole metre from the footplate.

Something else that was new to Grace, was a door in the side of the barn. She put her weight against the timber and it creaked open. Just behind her, Maddox peered over her head, and seeing that they were opposite a back entrance to the Thorndyke residence, he pointed the way with his own torch. Grace responded by unholstering her gun and crossing the short path to its porch and waiting there.

Heavy drizzle hit the inspector as he stepped out and within three strides he was kicking the farmhouse door open. Then Grace ducked inside on a tide of sleet, with the inspector at her back.

His bulk kept most of the weather at bay, then he eased the door shut, forcing out the storm and locking in an eerie silence.

The room was windowless and pitch black but Grace didn't think the light switch was going to be hit, leaving a crowd of partygoers to shout, 'SURPRISE!' at the top of their voices. Maddox turned his torch back on, but they saw no stairway; the only door was behind them and they'd just used it. The walls appeared to be panelled in wood, so Grace tapped on one with her knuckle. It sounded solid enough to her and as she scanned the darkness, their torch beams crossed over on an object at the centre of the room. A tripod stood in the space and both detectives were immediately drawn to the panel that its camera faced.

Grace took a breath and felt her way to the left-hand corner of the room, knocking as she went, while Maddox studied two candle holders on said wall. In his case, they were head height, set six feet apart and cold to the touch. Suspecting that each one was a handle, he gave them a gentle tug. The panel held on but he felt something give, so this time he pushed upwards as well.

All of this was being performed in the dark and suddenly, Maddox was aware of Grace on his left side, when her electric blue profile glinted at him. Escaping light from behind the pine board had seeped into their side and illuminated his protégé. Maddox lowered the false panel.

Chapter 51

Dominic watched his aunt dump Nathan's carcass in the pantry and shut the door as she came out. Why she handed him an onion on a stick, he couldn't think. Then the halfwit heard her sniggers as she washed her hands at the sink. He dropped the hat pin onto his dinner plate in disgust and chucked the whole lot into the waste.

Violet spoke first.

"Shake a leg, Nephew, we've got a busy night ahead."

His cruel imagination was doing somersaults and he envisaged the make-do skewer protruding from the back of her bristly neck as he passed behind her. Then, making sure he was beyond her reach, Dominic said, "What about the larder, Auntie Violet?"

She was double nasty tonight. "He'll keep, but get the old bath in case," she whined.

Chapter 52

Life is a river, the saying goes, and five days ago Grace had been paddling upstream in relative calm. The waters had become choppy in recent times but now she was entering rapids that churned and foamed.

Before her, the pine sheet dropped to reveal a scene that took her brain a good few seconds to decipher. Maddox strained under the weight of the timber, so long that it would cover a billiard table and with irises that had only now adjusted to the murky entrance hall, he too struggled with the appearance of a huge aquarium. Grace's first thoughts also prompted the idea of a massive fish tank, but rationale took over and she realised that behind the glass sheet, a turquoise glow from the right-hand side was casting an illusion of deep waters. A sigh of disbelief issued from her boss as he looked back to the video set-up and again at the two-way mirror. He saw that various trinkets in the room were picked out in blue from their right side, so that the faintest hint of figurine and picture frame emerged from shadow but fell back into shade on the objects' left side.

Nearer to the glass, lay the reason for the inspector's sorrow. Inexplicably, the first images that he focused on, were two rather pretty feet. Their soles faced an unusually high ceiling and the wrinkled skin was accentuated by the room's radiance. Now and again, he caught a glimpse of crimson nail varnish as they moved.

Buchanan's hand gun glinted as she holstered it and stepped nearer to the glass. At this end of the loathsome apparatus, Grace was closer to the girl's head. Letting her eyes follow the contours of a slim, pale physique, picked out by the blue haze, she traced the light along sinewy shoulders, past a curved spine, and felt a tear leaving her eye. She checked herself, then followed the glowing line up and around firm buttocks, where it dropped vertically to describe muscular calves and bleeding knees. Finally, she watched it taper down to ankles that were clasped into steel shackles. The rise and fall of the girl's back confirmed to Grace exactly what Maddox now whispered in her ear.

"She's alive." He leaned in to say something else, but Grace put a hand to his lips. Following her stare to the one-way glass, he saw a rectangle of white light open up on the far wall of the torture chamber.

Dominic Thorndyke was standing on the other side.

Rooted to the spot, the detectives watched him pick up a tin bath, before leaving the room with it. Then the chamber was shrouded in gloom again and his prisoner was squirming, like live bait in a snake trap. No sound escaped the glazing but from the evidence of her convulsions, the girl's screams were deafening and now they faced a dilemma. Break the glass and save the girl, or go after the brute and risk her life.

Grace had recognised an old sunbeam stove

through the open door and thought back to her first encounter with Mr Thorndyke. He'd tried to block her view as she sheltered from the rain, but she'd seen the oven two days ago and now Grace had gained a better perspective on the layout of the house.

Chapter 53

Nathan's indignities in death didn't end with an eye gouging and fractured skull. To go with them, he now had a broken nose, thanks to Dominic's clumsiness with the bath. He'd stood grinning at his handiwork until Violet's tuberous tone startled him.

"Put the wood in the hole, Dominic, and sit down, boy." His aunt had been acting strange lately, even for her, so after closing the door, the ingrate dragged a chair out at the opposite end of the table. She was in a cantankerous mood but only managed to look angry when she smirked.

"I bet you're itching to spend an evening with sexy Suzy, aren't you, Nephew?"

He dared to correct her. "It's Sophie, Aunt Violet!" Then he muttered, "Auntie… I haven't seen your meds lately!"

He saw the meat tenderiser in slow motion. It left Violet's hand like Hiawatha's tomahawk, turning over twice before settling into a more aerodynamic trajectory. For all of his experience with his aunt, the clod was never going to get out of harm's way and the steel mallet hit him square on the temple. By the time Violet had slammed the back door and stomped up the yard, Dominic was sporting what looked like a large marble under the skin of his left eyebrow. Vanity sent the pig rushing to the parlour to check out his injury in the mirror. He grimaced at the bruised ball, then saw Sophie's reflection and forgot all about his throbbing face.

Chapter 54

If they had hung around just one more minute, Grace could have introduced the inspector to the callous Mr Thorndyke in close-up, albeit through glass, but after extricating the camera's memory card, Maddox had ushered Grace and himself outside and into the waiting storm. She told him about the oven while he checked the safety on his weapon.

Jonathan Maddox couldn't help feeling protective of the young constable, he generally did with new recruits, but something about Buchanan made him even more sensitive and there was no way on earth that he'd ever leave her alone with the despicable Thorndyke. If anyone was going into that kitchen, it would be him and not some femme fatale. Grace guessed as much, but had no choice other than to obey his command, so went looking for another way into the farmhouse.

Chapter 55

The more Sophie tried to stop shaking, the worse it got for her. Dominic's clammy hands between the girl's legs had panicked her and now they slowly crawled their way up her inner thighs. Arachnid fingers playfully teased her, before the sadistic brute climbed onto a milking stool. The stricken girl heard him and dribbled like a baby as she clenched muscles that she never knew existed, focusing with every atom of her being on barring penetration. Her trembling excited Dominic, he preferred it when they resisted his advances, which many did. For this reason, he kept a good supply of Zanaflex and syringes in the parlour's bureau. The muscle relaxant was a last resort but Dominic thought he might need some tonight.

The animal had just stepped from the stool, when a beacon flashed in the corner. Sophie unclenched her buttocks and sucked some welcome air into her lungs as orange light filled the chamber. Earlier on, when the beacon flashed, her captor had left the room. Now he was pacing the floor and talking to himself. Sophie gathered from his mutterings, that he had an uninvited visitor. She listened to the sounds of him scuffling in a corner behind her, then probably the scraping of a drawer. Suddenly, the light went out and she heard a key rattling in a door.

Chapter 56

Stranded in the dark, the inspector held a breath and listened. After two strides into Thorndyke's kitchen, the fluorescent tube had tripped and now he wished he'd noted the exits. Then, in the blackness, cold steel touched his brow. Maddox instantly knew what it was, and out of the gloom, came an effeminate voice.

"That's a Purdy twelve gauge, in case you were wondering, Copper?" Dominic announced.

The barrel pinched some skin against Maddox's skull as the detective spoke.

"Mr Thorndyke, is this how you usually greet your guests?"

Dominic sneered at that and prodded harder with the shotgun. "What do you want with us at this time of night?" he hissed and Maddox sensed desperation in his tone, so baited him.

"Don't make this worse for yourself, Dominic." Hearing his own name mentioned unnerved the psychopath and Maddox could smell it.

Then, in one deft movement, while Dominic congratulated himself on keeping the parlour door lubricated, the inspector slid away from the barrel and brought his right arm upwards. The weapon fired into the ceiling and in that instant the flash illuminated the room and he saw the animal for the first time. Nathan would have appreciated the haymaker that felled Thorndyke but as he dropped, Maddox hoped he hadn't done too much damage, for with the blaze of gunpowder, came the realisation that Thorndyke had just said the word, 'US'.

Chapter 57

Outside, the rain had stopped and low cloud hugged the ground like dry ice on an X Factor stage. Grace watched it swirl as she searched the perimeter of the farmhouse. Here on the north side, most of the sash windows were on the second floor and she spotted one that looked open. Then, climbing a drainpipe to get onto the flat roof of an extension, Grace locked eyes with the rag doll again. She made her mind up, there and then, to find that room once and for all.

Chapter 58

When Dominic opened his eyes, he was staring at his aunt. She reclined non-seductively in the sunshine, across a chaise longue. Also in the monochrome photograph, sat her hated grandfather along with the bespoke wheelchair. Dominic's slumber had been disturbed by a sharp pain near his ankle and he knew exactly why. Maddox had over tightened the leather strap intentionally and was now fastening the other foot just as hard. The ingrate tried desperately to vent his anger but a third belt trapped his jaw onto a stirrup. Then, without warning, the cage of torture shook as if someone had thrown it down a mountain. The inspector had lifted Dominic inside his 'sexy wheelchair' and then dropped it from a height, onto the hard floor.

"How does it feel, Mr Thorndyke?" he asked, poking Dominic solidly on the forehead, and the fiend squirmed against his own personally designed constraints. Loosening the strap as he spoke, Maddox questioned him more.

"Who else lives here, Thorndyke?"

Noises coming from Dominic made him sound like a cornered animal, angrily wailing and spitting at the inspector.

"Hang around and you just might find out, you cunt!" he hissed back at him. Maddox could play hardball if needed, so reached for the shotgun. Then, using the heavily engraved butt, he compressed the marble-shaped bruise protruding from Thorndyke's eyebrow. Dominic's compliance was refreshing and he shouted the words.

"Auntie… it's my Aunt Violet… you fuck!"

Out of the parlour, Maddox felt much cleaner. Breathing the same air as Dominic Thorndyke turned his stomach so he closed the door on the creep. Then, hearing a noise from the pantry, he walked over, while taking a key from his trouser pocket. Earlier on, when he'd rescued Sophie, his main concern after finding some clothes and helping her dress had been keeping the girl safe. Straight away, he'd noticed the key in a door and persuaded her to hide and wait for him, suggesting she should make herself comfortable on an old tin bath.

Chapter 59

Movement in the cramped space was restricted, to say the least. Maddox had closed the pantry door against Sophie's toes and the bath's bottom rim was drawing blood from behind her thighs.

A musty and claustrophobic atmosphere was heightened further by darkness as Sophie cried for her mother and then, something cold grabbed her leg.

The poor girl's agony seemed endless and she cracked her head on a wooden shelf as she leapt away. With feet wedged between door and bath, something had to give and the loser was the galvanised tub. Then, Sophie elicited a whimper so soft, that she doubted her own hearing. Beside the bath, at her feet she watched a tear track its way from Nathan's good eye as her own dripped onto the dusty floorboards.

Chapter 60

Carpeted stairs helped dampen any sound from Grace's feet, once she'd squeezed through a small window and dropped, catlike, from the sill. Climbing the steps, she checked her surroundings. More dark panelling similar to the parlour's gave the hallway a sombre feel, which perfectly matched the mood of several large portraits hanging between the floodlit windows.

Grace was a great believer in the adage that, if you didn't laugh, you'd cry, and she mused about the architect of the house working his drawings in centimetres, before handing them to a builder who mistakenly converted the whole lot into inches.

Everything was so big and she could only manage one step at a time on the massive stairs. Water cascading down glass created fluid shadows that seemed to animate Thorndyke's ancestors, but Grace didn't see even a hint of Dominic's lineage. Although there appeared to be a family resemblance to each painting, it only went to prove that the Thorndykes hadn't made their fortune on the catwalk.

Another thing that the security beam brought to life, was at the top of the stairs. Leaning in a corner, a rustic-looking walking stick shimmered through the gloom. Grace touched the arts-and-crafts style carving and studied the gargoyle face. Being five foot eight in her socks, the constable was surprised that she had to look up to view its elaborate handle, but then casting her mind back to the wheelchair in the barn and some manacles hanging from a rafter, she concluded that the Thorndykes were avid collectors of all things macabre.

Ahead of Grace, where no light penetrated, a corridor branched off the balustraded landing to her right. She squinted into the dark space until a door on each side materialised at the end, certain that the right-hand one would lead to the rag doll.

Creeping slowly down the windowless tunnel, Grace asked herself why the hell she'd chosen a career in the police force. Before she could come up with an answer, the door was in front of her. Pushing it wide, she saw the rag doll in silhouette on the window's ledge, then it disappeared.

Thirty miles away, amongst black clouds over the town of Newmarket, an electrical storm was lighting the sky for miles around. Too distant for thunder to travel, it struck a second time and Grace saw the rosy-cheeked toy, plus a bed and some furniture. When the doll disappeared again, she felt for a light switch and flicked it… nothing… then lightning struck the heavens once more and Grace saw that the bulb was missing.

She also noticed another room to her left and more gloom beckoned her through a second door. It was only now, that Grace appreciated the scale of the opening, then pulling a cord for the light, she knew how Jack must have felt after climbing that beanstalk.

A Victorian bath stood centre stage, on four rococo feet, with ornate brass taps at one end. It was wide and long but the thing that alarmed Grace, was the fact that a children's rugby team could enjoy their after-match soak in it together. The en suite's dirty white tiles gave it the ambiance of a slaughter house and above Grace, suspended from the high ceiling, a chandelier projected her shadow into the bedroom as she stepped closer to the giant tub.

Recoiling at the thickest pubic hairs she'd ever come across, matted to a brown scum line, Grace turned and clapped eyes on the toilet. The huge bowl, obviously dreamt up by somebody large enough to need a bath the size of a small yacht, looked down from a two-foot-high platform. As she spun around, she felt something underfoot like chewing gum. Tugging her boot away, Grace saw that circling the bath, it appeared as though somebody had munched on some grapes and then spat tea-plate-size gloops of the horrible stuff onto the floorboards. Over time, a furry mould had grown and given it the patina of wet putty. Two more splats clung to the wall tiles and a sticky crimson residue dribbled from them.

Grace felt uneasy, surrounded by walls of grime in the abattoir-like bathroom, and was glad to get out. Its chandelier was very grand but any light escaping into the bedroom was limited to a triangle of yellow, just outside the door. Then, after forgetting all about the storm, it startled her as she reached the window, briefly showing more of the space. Again, darkness enveloped everything and she switched attention to a wardrobe on her right. She listened in the hush, waiting for the sky to ignite, and had the shock of her young life when it did.

Fortunately, the weapon aiming at her head was her own and she stared back at herself in a full-length mirror. Putting the Glock away, Grace took a pace nearer the wardrobe. The towering piece of furniture stood across a corner and a key in its lock, appeared to be handmade. She turned it and the thick timber creaked open to reveal more darkness.

Using the torch on her phone, Grace peered inside. The rail held five or six hangers and every one had a ladies' large tweed suit attached. She couldn't reach the rail so rummaged around in the bottom of the closet, finding the toe of a leather boot. Moving a hand in the gloom, she suddenly felt something run over it. Grace jumped out of her clammy skin, nearly crying out, before holding her nerve and realising that leather laces mimicked a rat's tail very convincingly.

The moment that Grace changed her mind about the macabre collection and decided that there could be a freak living at Cherry Tree Farm, happened when she lifted a hobnail boot, so big that she could've stood in the thing. She dropped it and stepped backwards, shining the torch around. Its beam hit the makeup-smudged face of another spooky doll on top of the wardrobe; this one was much larger and uglier. Then it winked at her and while she struggled to comprehend what had just happened, the wardrobe toppled over, pinning Grace to the floor.

Chapter 61

Downstairs, the kitchen resembled an A&E Department, with Nathan recumbent on a table, while Sophie tended his wounds. Maddox had a tap running and was soaking some towels, as she wrapped a torn sheet around her boyfriend's head. Then, the inspector handed her one and asked if she was OK. Sophie nodded a smile, afraid of how Nathan might react if he knew the truth. When she'd found him, he was incoherent and babbling about monsters and freaks, but Sophie had seen the ghoulish nightmare for herself, so was trying to reassure him when the inspector opened the pantry door.

At first, Maddox struggled to calm the girl, but he

soon coaxed a story from her, so fantastic that he hardly believed it. Now, content that the youngsters were out of immediate danger, he gave Sophie the shotgun and exited the kitchen via the narrow stairway to Dominic's bedroom.

Chapter 62

Rousing from her stupor, after being trapped by the neck, Grace entered a world of pain when she was dragged by her hair from under the wardrobe. To Violet, the policewoman was just a piece of meat and as she ripped her out of the gap, a jagged burr on the roughly formed key drew a deep gash along Grace's thigh. Violet ordered her to quiet down when she screamed, holding the woman aloft, as if she were a fisherman's proud catch.

Savouring the expression on a victim's horrified face, was one of Violet's few pleasures these days. They hardly ever struggled, which she put down to sheer terror, and Grace was no different. The constable made a vain attempt at recalling years of training but every muscle and sinew in her body just wanted to get away from the monstrosity that held her, if only she could stop shaking.

From this close, Violet's rank breath made Grace's eyes water, but she still noticed that the freak wore makeup. Garish tones of scarlet and orange mimicked the rag doll, and leathery skin stretched over bones that had never stopped growing. Grace Buchanan urged herself to face the monster, cringing at repulsively large nostrils, below close-set piggy eyes. Thorndyke stared back, raising one badly plucked eyebrow and grinning sarcastically. Then she drew Grace nearer to that grotesque skull and subdued her with chloroform.

To her nephew, torture and killing had become a leisure activity, whereas Violet found murder and the dispatch of a body to be a means to an end. Now she had a problem. The dead weight of that slut copper had to be dealt with before Dominic brought the entire Suffolk constabulary swarming over Cherry Tree Farm. She brushed away some lace curtains and scanned the yard. Rusting yellow paintwork of the shredder shone like a beacon to Thorndyke and Grace didn't even stir as the bed post bashed her ear on the way past.

She stayed that way, for every step down the stairs and across the deserted yard, until a biting draft grabbed the young woman and wrenched her from a vague slumber. Engulfed by the cold and darkness, Grace became aware of an alien sound competing against a howling wind. She imagined a washing machine on full spin, but today, it was her mum's copper saucepans that were on fast cycle. The noise got louder and louder until she was staring down an abyss that seemed to scream at her in a metallic language. Rattling steel repeated a rhythm and scratched out a syllable that echoed low inside the hollow chamber. It chimed again and again, but in Grace's tormented head, she heard the word 'DEATH' drummed over and over to the beat of her own heart and accompanied by a chorus of whirring, clunking gears. Icy steel scraped the back of an arm and Grace's stomach convulsed, the more her ears were assaulted and the deeper she was lowered. Then silence!

The machine had stopped. Only the ping of cooling metal and Grace's breathing disturbed the hush. Then a different noise interrupted the serenity. Violet Thorndyke cursed the contraption, before slamming Grace onto the concrete. Now, from within the depths of that damned hopper, it was the freak's shrill voice that echoed into the night and Grace guessed that it had jammed. Violet reached in and instantly located something that didn't feel mechanical. She tugged on it and was fortunate to clear the blades as they sprung into life again.

In the days to come, star-filled skies would bring this night vividly back to life for Grace Buchanan. The young woman would mostly recall the time when, spread-eagled on her back with the moon in her eyes, she kicked out at Thorndyke from under the shredder. In doing so, she caught the ogre above both ankles and shifted the freak's balance, causing Violet to stumble, flailing for something to prevent her fall. Luckily for Grace, that something was one of the shredder's twenty-four hammers. As Violet touched it, a second hammer smashed her knuckles, followed by a third on her wrist, then a fourth and a fifth… a sixth…

By the time she pulled the hand out, it was mush.

While Violet studied the jagged skin flaps at the end of her forearm, Grace hauled herself off the floor using the handle of a rake. Tilting her throbbing head upwards, she eyed the beast. From below, Violet's nostrils were even more impressive and some bristly hair grew out of them, long and thick. At the ends, mucus collected and like rain clouds that get too heavy, they shed their load and dripped into Grace's upturned pupils. It stung like hell and as she wiped them, she could hear Thorndyke howling like a baby. Then Grace felt the rake tug at her hand and opening one eye, she saw it scything the air towards her.

In that moment, the planet seemed to be in freeze frame and Grace felt as if she'd looked deep into the soul of Violet Thorndyke. When, upon those revolting lips, a smile formed that spoke of contentment and relief. At exactly the same time, something else developed, but this was on Violet's bony forehead. A ten-centimetre hole opened up between that monobrow and deerstalker hat, oozing a thin line of blood that trickled between her eyes.

Those eyes didn't show pain, but instead, Grace saw peace, as years of anger and frustration were forgotten and Violet finally left this world of torture behind. The exit hole wasn't quite so tidy and most of her abnormal brain decorated a metal sign that read, 'WELCOME TO CHERRY TREE FARM'.

Chapter 63

The way Violet Thorndyke keeled over was more reminiscent of one of the giant spruces on her land being felled, than a middle-aged lady suffering a headshot from a large-calibre hand gun. After losing her grip on the rake, and spraying brain tissue on anything within two metres, the monster's eyes closed and her colossal skeleton shook the ground beneath the boots of both detectives as it whacked the concrete.

Maddox wanted to pump another round into the grotesque thing at his feet, but Grace stopped him with a tentative hand. They stared at it for an eternity under floodlight, mulling over the giant wheelchair and bath, before turning around to face the house.

Chapter 64

Inside the kitchen, Grace kept her cool and tried to assess the injuries of two young people on a large table. Maddox contacted Bury station to confirm one fatality and arrange ambulances, plus a meat wagon for Dominic.

The young woman mumbled something to the constable but wasn't making much sense. Frustration was etched on the girl's face so Grace reached out to her. She was cheered by this and jumped down from the table. Then, grabbing Grace's arm, she led her to a waste bin behind some curtains under the sink. It was overflowing with empty sandwich packs and Coke cans but the girl only showed interest in a steel pin, which she slid out from one of the boxes. If there was a gentler way for Sophie to illustrate Nathan's situation to the constable, then she might have taken it, but time was their enemy now. Remarkably, Grace hid her shock quite well at the appearance of a human eyeball, and placed it inside a Tupperware container from the fridge.

When Maddox drew his Glock, she followed suit by gently taking the shotgun out of Sophie's trembling hands. Then, with his shoulder against the parlour door, Maddox asked her if she was prepared. A determined look in Grace's eye, and the butt of the Purdy rammed hard into an armpit, told him that she was ready, so he twisted the brass handle. The door eased inwards and Maddox followed it, as Grace leant in to hit the light switch, before stepping through behind the shotgun. The scene in front of them, didn't really equate. Logic informed the detectives of a totally different scenario. But there it was, no other statement would suffice.

The cage was empty!

Chapter 65

The next day, at the station, backs were patted and hands were shaken a little too much for Maddox's liking, but he was glad of Grace's company at the debrief. Sarge told her that Dominic had vanished into thin air and that all of the properties he visited when supporting the elderly, had been searched and given the all-clear, although there was information to suggest that he'd been trying on some of the old dears' clothes. More evidence on the creep's mobile phone didn't really shock Grace and he was already categorised as a voyeur anyway. What did surprise her, was Dominic's hatred for his aunt. He'd obviously taken photos of her sleeping, and then uploaded the pictures onto an illegal fetish site. Studying the naked snaps, Grace looked deep inside herself and found a trace of empathy for Violet Thorndyke. Then, all at once, she understood the huge relief and solace that became etched onto the leatherish face of the desperate freak, as realisation dawned and that massive heart stopped beating.

Chapter 66

Two months later

After hours of uninterrupted blue sky, the sun tried to hide behind cotton wool clouds that seemed to queue in front of a panoramic window. Blown along from right to left, they marched across a stunning Norfolk landscape, framed by curtains of out-of-date chintz. Wind on the east coast could be ferocious at any time of the year but it was Dominic's favourite place anywhere on Earth. Taking in the captivating view, he reminisced about the old days. Running down dark hallways as a child, always just out of reach of his chasing aunt. It was only now, sitting in Mrs Jackson's caravan, that he realised Violet could have caught him whenever she chose. She'd toyed with the boy, terrorising him, and the resulting anger he felt at this moment simmered and bubbled like a saucepan about to boil over, and the lid was rattling.

As bolt holes go, it wasn't bad at all. Unbeknown to Mrs Jackson, the old girl had spent her late husband's life insurance on a six-berth caravan at Golden Sands holiday park, keeping up the site payments for over twelve years until Dominic's rainy day had finally come. Eight weeks had passed since he'd witnessed Violet's demise and with October here, the seaside hamlet would turn into a ghost town. That suited him perfectly. The high street struggled because of this, and so charity shops took their opportunity like jungle vines, seeding themselves on the branches of weakened trees and then strangling their host. Not that he needed to watch the pennies, of course. Dominic had become a specialist in bleeding his old ladies dry. Their savings were targeted first, but very subtly. Then, one of his favourite tricks was to replace a valuable trinket with a cheaper object and sell the good one. It could be a figurine or an old clock but the safest way was to find something valuable in the back of a drawer and he had spent his whole career rummaging through clients' private property. Fortunately for the pensioners of England, Dominic's days in the care industry were finished and they could get a peaceful night's sleep, without him tipping a cup of water on their nether regions or popping an empty crisp packet by their ear.

Dementia in adults covers a massively broad spectrum, which leads to infinite levels of the cruel illness. In the case of Ivy Jackson, as with a lot of sufferers, her long-term memory was slightly better than her short-term. She had a cheerful disposition and always looked forward to holidays with her lovely support worker, Dominic. Unfortunately, every moment of clinging to that thought, was followed by another moment of forgetting it and for that precise reason, Ivy presented the ideal candidate to the devious bastard that Thorndyke was.

A lot of her fortnight's vacation was spent sitting on the caravan's toilet. It didn't matter that she was incontinent, so after taping some absorbent pads to the seat, Dominic would undress her and secure the old girl by her ankles. Then, as long as he kept her reasonably fed and flushed the loo now and again, she was quite happy, leaving him to work on his future lair. The first thing to be installed, was a state-of-the-art air conditioning system normally fitted to the sailing boats of the wealthy. Then he set about converting the place into something more befitting of a madman, hellbent on inflicting pain on the female race.

Chapter 67

The scene through the caravan's end window, afforded Dominic not a landscape or indeed a seascape, but a skyscape. At the bottom of the picture, the North Sea was blocked out by a concrete promenade, the longest on the east coast. For three weeks now, that vista had become Dominic's world, transforming into the biggest widescreen ever. After weeks spent trawling the Internet, Dominic's base carnal urges still refused to be satiated. The creature would have to find his entertainment elsewhere. Unpolluted sea air and smooth concrete devoid of traffic were a magnet for health nuts and runners, so Dominic's days were filled with an endless procession of pink and tanned flesh. He'd settled into a predictable routine of waking before sunrise to scurry through the dim light and buy his daily intake of sandwiches and wraps. Then he would sit at the window for hour upon hour, people watching. During this period, the psychopath developed a morbid fascination for the comings and goings of various characters on the prom and quite a little soap opera had played out before him. Some of them, he could set his clock by, and he would generally see them twice a day. Firstly on their way out, then back again. A lot of the joggers nodded hello to each other and walkers were friendly enough. Dominic considered it a success if two strangers stopped opposite his window to pass the time of day. Sometimes, he craved a freeze-frame facility when the sporty bitches sprinted past with their pumped arms and defined shoulders. Although to him they were just soft porn, merely an appetiser to the hardcore stuff. Thorndyke needed to see real suffering in the eyes of a conquest, leading to fear and the ultimate thrill of a female begging for her life.

Plain Janes were more his style and once a week,

just such a type strolled the walkway before sitting down to read a book. She ticked nearly all of the boxes for Dominic, in a criteria that would allow him to sustain an erection for any length of time. A female couldn't be too attractive in any way. Self-confidence would not be tolerated, nor did he seek a conversationalist. They also had to be slim and fair-skinned, but there was a deal breaker. Dominic only considered redheads.

Compared to the rest of the cast, Daisy, as he'd named her, was a newcomer to the show and Dominic had studied the girl, listing her talents and making his usual vulgar entries. She was categorised as compliant, virginal and narrow hipped. He also made a special note about the way her backside spread out as she sat on the sea wall. Daisy always wore a heavy beige coat with a matching belt. She fastened it tight and left the end to flap in the wind. A red fringe protruded from her crocheted hat and more wisps of ginger curled out near the girl's cheekbones. This highly restrained ensemble was topped off by a pair of very sensible brown loafers.

Dominic had introduced himself three days ago. He'd stood on the low wall with some binoculars and pretended to look at the horizon. Then, as she'd sneaked a glance at him, he called out to her, saying how dramatic the sky was today. That was enough to start with so he waited a few days and now it was time for stage two. He sat as near to Daisy as he dare, elbows on knees as if in thought. His peripheral vision was excellent and it wasn't long before he noticed her spying on him. He took his chance.

"A bit fresh, don't you think?" The wind took his words.

"Sorry, what was that…? It's so windy!" She leant towards him to hear. Dominic shifted to his right.

"The weather, it's…" He smiled. "It's a bit windy."

They both laughed at their awkwardness and then the pair of them looked out to sea.

Stage three would have been for another day, if Daisy hadn't mentioned using the facilities. Pointing to the toilet block along the promenade she apologised but said she had to dash. Dominic jumped on this and suggested that it would be silly to go all that way to use a public convenience, when she was quite welcome to use his. The beast watched her, as she lingered for what seemed an age and then timidly accepted his invitation, following him down a sandy ramp and across a patch of grass. Dominic opened the door so that Daisy might climb the two small steps into his humble abode, offering her a polite hand.

Chapter 68

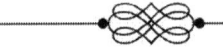

When the door closed behind her and the bolt slid in its lock, Grace was more disappointed than surprised. Disappointed in herself for thinking that she could get away with it but still not sure if Thorndyke knew who he had snared. Sadly, she wouldn't find that out until after the effects of the Halothane vapour had worn off and all of this ran through the constable's mind as the floor came rushing towards her. Just before the Lino smacked Grace's face, she wondered at what point Dominic had recognised her, then it was lights out.

For seven painful weeks, she'd lived on a diet of protein, vitamins and water, to lose the twenty-eight pounds that would give her a slighter frame. It had worked great and she had gone the full Monty by having her hair cut and dyed red. Partnered with a pale toner and freckles, plus the dowdy clothes, Grace thought she had done a convincing job. After a day sifting Dominic's disgusting bedroom, she felt like she'd been inside his head and knew exactly what type of woman he lusted after.

Herself and Maddox had been given involuntary paid leave, once the dust had settled on Cherry Tree Farm, but that meant handing in all firearms. The inspector travelled to see family in New Zealand, which left Grace to drown her sorrows at the local wine bar. Two hangovers, plus a one-night stand later, and her teeth started to itch.

She located Thorndyke relatively easily, now that she'd explored the workings of his sordid mind, quickly realising that his profession was just a money tree and his old ladies were there to be exploited. Trailing him without her gun concerned Grace but she'd taken on men like Thorndyke and come out on top many times.

Chapter 69

Outside, Dominic made his way to the back of the caravan, while removing a capsule from his top pocket. Breaking the end, he placed it inside the vent of an air-conditioning unit. Then slipping a military-grade gas mask on, he used the real door to enter the caravan.

Thorndyke was in no doubt as to the identity of the woman at his feet. The filth's biggest mistake was spotted through some high-powered binoculars, earlier in the week. A second day on page eleven of her paperback could have been put down to slow reading, but a third day looking at the same words got his hackles up and the rose-tinted glasses were off. He couldn't believe his own gullibility but went ahead with the plan, anyway.

Grace's nose made a wet clicking sound as Dominic's heel broke it, while stepping over her on his way to one of the bedrooms. The old master suite had probably seen some action through the years but seaside romance didn't immediately come to mind, when Grace looked through Thorndyke's legs as he opened the door. With bleary eyes stinging from tears and blood seeping into the corner of her mouth, it swung shut again, but not before she saw an image projected onto the entire end wall of his playroom.

Grace had two seconds to digest a scene that she'd been trying to wipe from her memory banks for the last eight weeks. Using the caravan's end panel like a mini cinema, Thorndyke was showing a film of the infamous sex cage at the farm. In the brief viewing, Grace failed to register the two stars of the film but had a good idea as to the identity of the person who wasn't restrained in the apparatus.

The room had stopped spinning and for a minute, Grace's arms didn't feel entombed inside a lead-weighted diver's suit, so she took a chance to survey her surroundings. The iron bars that had trapped her when she'd entered, were now set aside in their runners, for a more homely atmosphere. In this area of the chalet, where meals would normally be taken, another one of Thorndyke's imaginative inventions took pride of place. While Grace pondered its use, the playroom door opened and Dominic filled the space. The rubber straps of his mask were too tight and pinched the fiend's skin into blotchy ridges. As she succumbed to the effects of the gas again and drifted away, the picture that Grace took with her, was of Dominic Thorndyke in that green mask, standing naked and erect.

Chapter 70

Two hours later, a bitter chill made Grace reach for her toes. Though it did her no good, because she couldn't move. Then it dawned on the woman, that Thorndyke had stripped and manacled her to one of his contraptions. What she couldn't know, was that as her eyes brought into focus two panting bodies on the giant screen in front of her, the rest of her naked self was behind the wall, in the other room, and the stabbing ache Grace felt in her neck was from the jagged edge of a crude hole cut into the partition. She didn't recognise the screaming female in the movie but the man raping her and looking sideways at the camera, was definitely Thorndyke. Behind Grace, on the other side of the wall, a cool draft confirmed that she was undressed and made her think back to the girlfriend of Travis Brown going up those stairs.

With lids tightly shut, she forced her own cold limbs to read the landscape of her incarceration, as if it were braille. Veins pumping adrenaline around her body enhanced Grace's senses tenfold and in her mind, she saw stirrups of leather and rusting metallics. At the forefront of Grace's imagination, was an uncomfortable picture of something fitted to her pubic bone, over her thighs and around the coccyx. It wasn't painful, but whatever was spreading Grace apart, had her in its grip, physically and mentally. She had never experienced such vulnerability and felt safer in the other room, so opened her eyes again.

The sight that met them was so close that Grace struggled to focus at first. When the brute slowly materialised, shaven and semi-hard, she flinched. Thorndyke laughed at her, squatting down so that their noses nearly touched and Grace realised that he had gagged her, as she attempted to bite the bastard. He laughed again and flicked her broken nose, before rising to his feet and speaking for the first time since she'd been there.

"Not quite Nicole Kidman, but nice try, Miss Buchanan." Only then, did Grace recollect the gas mask, as Thorndyke continued.

"You let me down in other places, so I took the liberty of using the razor on them, if that's alright?" Grace struggled in her harness but all that she managed to accomplish, were deep scratches above her shoulders from the serrated edge of the hole. Dominic moved to the door on tiptoes.

"Why don't you settle down and enjoy the film? It's a classic!" She couldn't see him but heard the handle.

"See you on the other side, Grace." The door opened and closed.

With a red glare from the make-do screen being the only source of light, Grace expected to be immersed in sunshine when the door opened, but it was obviously night time and she reasoned that the gas Thorndyke used had to be serious stuff. She closed her eyes yet again and left the cinema. On the other side, Grace felt the faintest rise in temperature as Thorndyke approached her. She jumped at his touch on her calf and suddenly understood the monster. He had put himself in a world of darkness like his victim, so that they might experience everything together. Grace swallowed as slimy fingertips dug into the crease at the back of her knee and then slowly progressed up her trembling thighs.

The next thing she was aware of, totally threw her. A delicate smack on her right buttock made Grace pinch her eyelids together in the hope of discerning what it could be. When she sensed two more near her anus and another on her leg, Grace envisioned dripping wax. If her ears weren't in the other room, she might have heard the sound of metal to go with the wet dribbling noise. Another unfamiliar sound would have been the slurping of Dominic's tongue as it was pinned to the roof of his own mouth by the wide blade of a butcher's knife. The intended path of the steel, when rammed up through his chin, was deflected slightly and exited Thorndyke's septum, just above his top lip. Rather fortuitously, it sliced the tip of his nose off as it went by. The final symphony that Grace might have enjoyed, happened in a flash. The glinting blade was withdrawn, then returned on a much shallower angle. This time it was thrust behind the nasal cavity and deep into the brain of the last surviving Thorndyke. The *drip, drip, drip* that had confused Grace so much, was now a torrent of Dominic's warm blood and it cascaded onto her spine, collecting in the hollow, before running between the woman's buttocks and down her legs. Grace's mind was in utter turmoil and the tears that she'd held back as the door burst inwards, left her as a pitiful sob when Jonathan Maddox loosened the gag and removed the ball from her mouth.

After that, he took her face in his hands and kissed her eyes. They remained that way until flashing blue lights filled the windows and bathed them in their welcome glow.

ABOUT THE AUTHOR

Keith James Sargeant, 55 years of age and care worker. Married to Janet, with a son named Rhys.

First attempt at writing was a children's story called *Krakal-spark*. Has a passion for art, in all of its forms and enjoys drawing, watercolour and sculpture.

Printed in Great Britain
by Amazon